FOREWORD

What I scribbled so many years ago in my cousin Luis' Brooklyn apartment was a sloppily written urban parable at best. Something I later rediscovered and decided to tweak until it manifested into its' own beast. A few have opined on drafts over the years misunderstanding the tales' intent. The parallelism between the unapologetic magical realism and a traditionally discarded urban underbelly was offensive, as was the actuality of cause. Unquestionably the tale is dark. "sin of the forgotten" needs the soil of its' actions to be slowly cupped in order to truly disinter the restless and voiceless.

There was a time when New York City was choking on discarded crack vials and needles. People dealt, used, and died. Some made it through, thankfully, finding feasible blessings and negotiated augury.
As you read this first story, ponder the causes, the why. To believe that indifference and iniquitousness are motherless is akin to hiding under a blanket of naivety. Remember that broken entities often manifest brittle or unintentional magic.

sin of the forgotten

BY CARRIÓN GRIMES

ISBN: 978-1-7374662-0-8

Library of Congress Control Number: 2022944196

First Printed Edition 2023

Editor: Aden Suchak

Editor: Melissa D. Scardina

Book design & Images: Alcides Cervantes "Akira"

Cover based on image by: Minelsa Del Rosario

Inside images based on cinematography by James Usmanov

Published by:

Helmet Free Media, LLC

127 West 83rd Street New York City, NY 10024

www.Helmetfreemedia.com

Appreciation

I appreciate all those who supported this project. Lourdes C for so much unsaid, Milagros for pointing me in the right direction, Taisha M for opening the doors and walking me through, Roland G for the constructive criticism, Tina Marie, Luis RS always, Luis AS, Carlos, Damien S, Jessica, Melissa, Al, Jose, Veronica D, Maria TU for all the transcribing. Thanks to all those who read the countless drafts. Thank you all.

"IF YOU CHANGE THE WAY YOU LOOK AT THINGS, THE THINGS YOU LOOK AT CHANGE." W.D.

the names i remember…

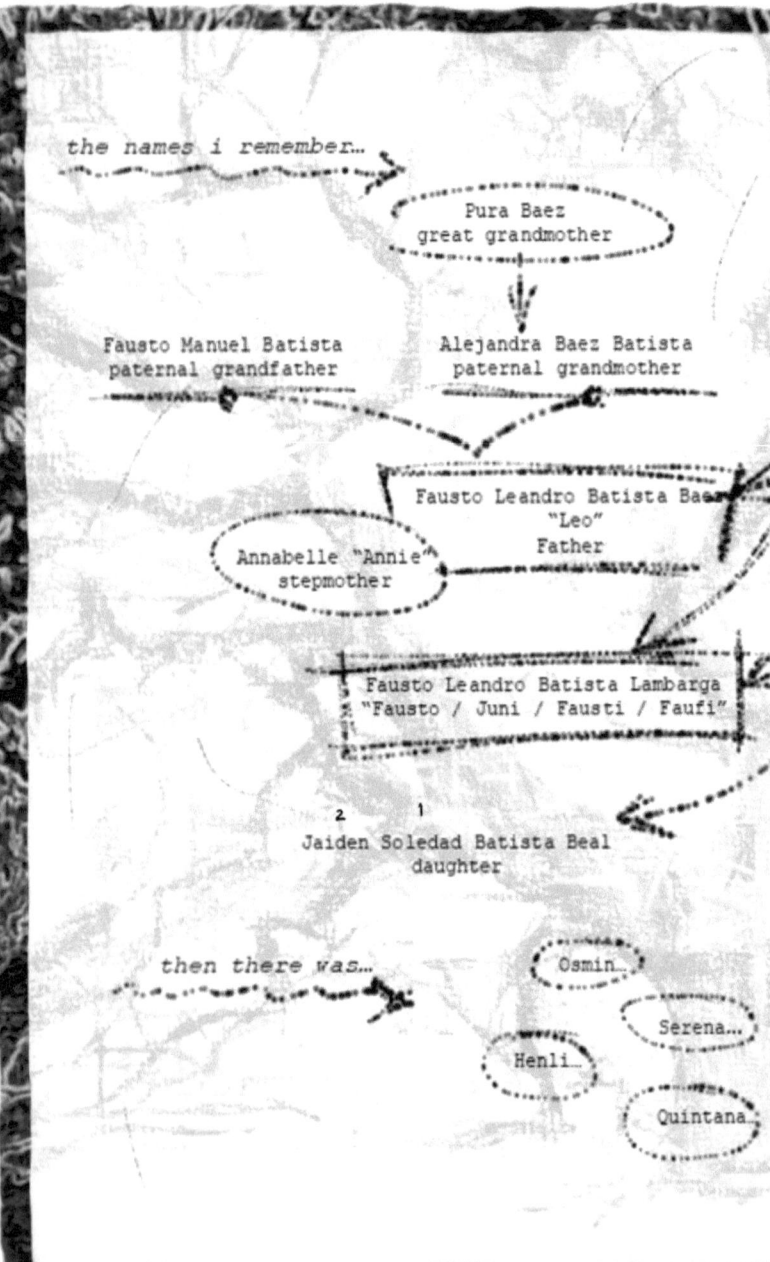

Pura Baez
great grandmother

Fausto Manuel Batista
paternal grandfather

Alejandra Baez Batista
paternal grandmother

Fausto Leandro Batista Baez
"Leo"
Father

Annabelle "Annie"
stepmother

Fausto Leandro Batista Lambarga
"Fausto / Juni / Fausti / Faufi"

2   1
Jaiden Soledad Batista Beal
daughter

then there was…

Osmin…

Serena…

Henli…

Quintana…

General Reynaldo Lambarga
maternal great grandfather

Berenice
maternal great grandmother

Reynaldo Lambarga Soler
maternal grandfather

Bellamaria Soler Lambarga
maternal grandmother

Yolandamari Lambarga Batista
"Yoli"
Mother

Angela Gianni Beal Batista
"Angie"

Nati Mirabal Beal
mother

Norton Beal
father

Ifita...

Leni...

Papito...

Margaro...

...But there were more.

"Things fall apart: the center cannot hold:

Mere anarchy is loosed upon the world,

The blood-dimmed tide is loosed, and

everywhere;

The ceremony of innocence is drowned;

The best lack all conviction,

while the worst

Are full of passion intensity"

The Second Coming

William Butler Yeats

CHAPTER 1

breath hesitant and exhausted

"My pants crudely cut,

sweeping along the soil,

sliding over the calluses at my heels.

I step passed past graves to the left,

then right.

Toenails curving,

Gasping for a taste of the air that no longer

mattered,

they who are dead lay over boxes

covered over with dirt

disturbed.

Bodies beneath.

Waiting,

hands crossed,

index to shoulder.

Index to shoulder.

I want to reach and feel their soles, but alas the

crimson hovel sees me,

I hear its' breathing,

I stand at the threshold. I'm here."

...THEY DEAD

CHAPTER 2

Digits fully extended, its' silver rings tinking against a door that sighs as it opens less than enough. Impressed dirt from years of unwash stain the edge, a doorknob survives, but only as a stem.

Inside smells only of camphor and mold, naught light.

> *cough.*
>
> *cough.*

Something rustles along the floor, going silent then thumping into a rustle once more.

Then.

The lamp flickered on and intensified, the Bell Howell as it ruptured the black. Its' hum igniting sparsely dispersed tapers that before longfully dozed, every one clothed in spider's silk and delicately adorned in dust.

Each speckled with paint, their points dull.

Like Bernoulli's lemniscate, a lone one arcs, then
swings.
The rope that cradles one, the suspended one,
is made of twined and stained cloth scraps
leading to a
lightlessness
that conceals an end.
She rubbed her eyes.

un congo!
"i see him."

His back, hulking, pressing to where the walls
met. Shadows shifting, irritably, in
stressed candlelight as five gathered in Ifita's
common space.
Orishas.

Almost irascibly, they wait.

The old woman who it belongs to,

and her to it,

this little red house with the unfinished doors,

weathered.

She,

serenely rocking in her mahogany chair. Trapped
sand crackling under the curved wood.
Inches near, a rooster engaged in futile,
desperate hopping, briefly searching for its'
head before she snatched it up and made use
of the blood. The undefined globules spotting
the coconut sections she'd tossed to the
ground moments before.

A crouched angel stares at her from
underneath the folding table in hopes that their
eyes will meet. Perhaps she'd then make use of
her opuele,

     for it is a beginning and an end.
But the old woman is uninterested in urgencies
or the tarnished divining chain. Rushing has a
cost,

     before.
She remembered memories that she'd

neglected to forget.

As a girl, she'd embraced the cowrie shells.

The Orisha, Yemaya, loved her.

Since birth she would arrange the little

porcelain-like seashells,

> *pretty little things,*

on the ceiling above her makeshift bassinet so

the child would learn to divine even in her sleep.

When Orunla became aware of what,

> *of what!?*

his wife had freely given to a child, the demi-

god made it so that the shells always landed

faced down, ensuring they could not be

interpreted. Yemaya's gift, however, had been

too well given, and Ifita learned to foretell on

her own substituting pop-tops for shells.

The practice of astragalomancy arrived at her

on the day she left Haiti, this was long before

the Milice Volontaires de la Sécurité Nationale,

> *tanton macoute.*

It was when François Duvalier was only a doctor,

before he cosplayed bawon samdi

and acquired the nickname,

in the mid-morning midst of the négritude
movements' poetry, when America's beloved
beige ruled the island nation. Estimé was gaining
popularity and swelling the expectations that
would lead him to the presidency. And usher in
the reign of a doctor turned dictator,

the reign of papa doc.

It was barely dawn when she chose to no longer
be anyone's restivik and the morning she traded
the Madame's heaviest silver for a ride. Her pre-
pubescent body wedged between the sweaty
driver and two women who had grown too fat
and paid too little for their perfumes.

She watched them tear meat from drumsticks
and wings,

the glistening slivers of charcoal grilled skin
briefly wiggling between their lips, she grew
hungrier.

Decades prior this road was the river's bed.

Despite its' resolve it was damned, and only its'
ghosts lingered, buried, in stones partially risen,
making the truck bang then bump.

Peeking briefly at his side mirror the driver
licked his filthy chicken flavored fingers in
satisfaction and then adjusted his rearview so
to better view the first woman who had grown
too fat, or, more specifically the buttons
laboring to restrain her mammaries. Welcoming
the attention, the first woman,

who had grown too fat,

extended then pursed her lips, inhaled, and
looked away.

She stretched her neck back against the seat's
edge where the headrest would have been if
there had there been a headrest. Her friend
took the under-witnessed opportunity to shoot
a look at the driver, her greased lower lip
sensually sliding forward beneath her front
teeth to meet its' fraternal twin.

then.

In an effort to muffle it, Ifita pressed her palms against her rumbling belly, her eyes darted around the truck's cabin.

"for what you looking about child," the driver asked his voice deep and unsmooth.

"driver, i think her want chicken,"
said the second woman
who had grown too fat.

His unusually long calloused finger pointing,

"you must speak child, when you want to be heard you must be loud... scream if you have to, but let all know that you have words to say. if you do you no feel bad or no hungry no more. And your tummy be full now instead of growling at my bones?"

Ifita looked down at the discarded bones. In their arrangement they spoke.

The communication came in still flashes and undertone, fragments really, held together by

nothing but their order. The message she
divined warned her.

get away... run... now!

from the truck,

from the road.

Frightened, she mumbled towards the driver, he
could not hear her over the plump breasts of
the first woman,

who had grown too fat.

She screamed, as if menaced by the death until
he stopped nearly sending those in the back off
the truck.

Ifita screamed.

"turn around... leave the truck."

Angrily the driver pierced with his eyes.

her.

With neither a breeze nor the vehicle's motion
the women,

who had grown too fat,

fanned themselves with displeasure, but he only

grew enraged as she continued to voice. With one fluid movement he plucked her up and flung her off the truck. Blood marked the stone where her knee landed.

With wet eyes, her head turned back, only to be pelted with the bones as she tried to stand.

> "we have already crossed
>
> you stupid, stupid child...
>
> you walk... let the goat catch you!"

The truck launched dust and rocks as it pulled away. She quickly picked up the bones and ran into the trees. Afraid, she wandered them until the Sun warmed too much and her knee grew too swollen. She sat, and then, waited, the heated air making her drowsy.

Pain leapt to her abdomen from her knee as she slept. The sound of hard rain bashing against corrugated metal echoed in the distance. The air yet was not wet.

Unknowingly, that eve she began her first flow.

Her eyelids flickering into wanted surroundings,

happiness and abundance,

vague to her.

The smell from the bones made her hollow.

When it overtook, it awoke her.

She sucked the bones, and ravenously savored the saliva and marrow. From above, a serpent hung leering at her, unwilling to know her it recoiled.

Coconuts lay fallen on all sides of her, she picked one and felt its' milk stir, but as thirsty as she was, the stones she slammed against it were not successful in releasing even the littlest drop. Ifita suspected they were soft stones as a result of being far too ripe. She placed a pebble under her tongue and walked.

When the dimming day cooled the air, Ifita made her way to the road. Voices were loud, she dared not step onto it. She chose to move, cautiously, within the brush as she watched two of the Goat's soldiers joking as they strenuously rolled the corpse of one of the ladies,

who had grown too fat,

onto the back of the truck. They then got in and
drove towards more soldiers in automobiles that
waited some distance up. They were under the
Goat's orders to hate the Haitians,

and,

they did.

Trujillo or the Goat as called behind his back,

who the hell knows why,

was a brutal dictator.

His cruelty and societal control neared an august
omnipotence.

The Dominican Republic was once rather brutally
annexed by Haiti, but that was before the birth
of grandmothers, a bloodletting old and often
remembered as needed. Now the warmed blood
of Haitians poured like discarded bathwater.
Ifita's Papa would whisper to her that the
dictator's grandmother had been Haitian, she
believed him then, now it did not matter.

A neighbor said he had traveled to a Petit Haiti in the United States.

But he was missing now, many said that he was among the twenty thousand who could not pronounce parsley,

> *perejil.*

> *a misappropriated lesson.*

It didn't matter, he was not there. A thrust of air wrapped over her, it was rich with the scents of cheap perfume and blood. The smell saddened her so that she cried, quietly, she moved behind the tree. There she was sure she had been heard. With both hands over her mouth Ifita stood motionless until the Earth had rolled passed the light. Then, her bones tightly in hand, she ran until it again arrived.

At random moments in the day she still smelled the cheap perfume. It reminded her to trust the dead driver's chicken bones more than any other tools of divination. As years went on, countless sought her to obtain the truths behind their problems. Some even enhanced her other abilities in exchange for her assistance. Tonight would not be different.

But it was many years later.

and she was old.

The creased black skin on her face sagged off cheeks that moved slightly out of rhythm with the chair. Her cartoonish mouth twisted and puffed as her unmoistened lips wrapped around her crooked hand rolled andullo. The locally grown strain was a chewing tobacco and was not intended for smoking, which was evident as the ashes continued to glow hot even after they hit her floor near where the slain bird lay fallen. With the last few puffs of a cigar, the bones would tumble onto the table and the future would unfurl before them. The thick plume would lift,

eventually,

and they'd see.

All sensed it would be a disquieted night,

still,

she could not be warned.

A river of souls forgotten under the stars

smothered light could listen.

Ochun too often spoke as she slumbered.

dense whisperings.

Nothing as before.

...TI FI PEDI

CHAPTER 3

"reality will always dance to a crying child's serenade."

In a place of brittle amens, the building they lived in was brown and grungy.

Eight stories of aged bricks held together as much by dirt as by the century plus old mortar used to lay them. The entrance,

> *illumined from an angle by a memorial consisting of a baker's dozen saint adorned wax filled glasses and photos affixed to a makeshift lowercase t's, maybe it was a cross,*

was identical to most tenements around the city in that it met with the street, but from the left side and rear it and its' siblings were notably distinct in how they stood as much on the earth as above it.

Oxidizing fire escapes stitched their way around

the edifice, and it rested on one-hundred-foot
beams that thrusted powerfully into the ground.
A dinky two-door entrance expanded to an
unpolished marble lobby that showcased worn
remnants of a prestigious past. On either side of
the grand hallway two majestic, gray-speckled
mirrors stood over defunct fireplaces etched
with ivy, a theme continued through the semi-
circular staircases, stenciled shadows of pilfered
decorations impressed the walls. The
centerpiece was a fresco of a young Flamenco
dancer surrounded by six men. Under decades of
grime and graffiti, the young woman's dejected
eyes were still surveying her visitors.

> *don't really gotta be too nice...*
> *whole neighborhood turned shitty*
> *once they came...*
> *them people don't know good.*

Along the walls the lugubrious neshamot of the
elderly made their way along the interior,
their right hands pressed flat against the cracked

plaster and paint,

their heads weighed by loneliness, and disregard.

Their Heights,

belonged to the past,

       as did their memories.

Passed them,

the hallways trapped the smells of handed-
down Latin seasonings and cooking along with a
musty mixture of diluted lemon-floor-cleaners
too weak to properly remove the generations
of entrenched filth and ever replenishing piss.
The elevator shrank every few years as the
landlord added new paneling and tiling over the
old to create the illusion of modernization in
this tragedy awaiting opportunity. The sixth
floor was repainted-over heavily to smother the
chipping lead-based original layers.
The volume on the babysitters could be heard
through the metal doors,

       commercials and all.

As the flickering lights buzzed above, the elevator doors opened.

He staggered out, giggling to himself, and headed towards the apartment. Gulping then coughing he tossed down the bottle, to his surprise it did not shatter. Squeezing one hand into a fist he rested his shoulder against the door.

With a soft knock and taunting hushed speak,
"yooooli. yoooooooooli. come on. mami! abrame la puerta please."
Softly she slid the peephole cover and tried not to breathe as she stared upon him.

"negra come onnnnn, open the door," sensing her close.
Legs extended Yoli sat on the floor near the door, she longed to hear his voice say her name,
the way he used to say it.

that was also passed.

Memories of his touch made her,

made... her...

well, that don't matter now.

She knew better than to open. Her son sleepily stumbled into the hallway, and she motioned for him to go to bed. Her teeth clenched as her wrist clicked from a recent fracture. It was late and he was accustomed to the ruckus, it frequented their home at least once a week, he was five.

"yol... yoli... mami come on... don't be like that...
coño yoli!"

His forearm slamming against the door.

"deja tu baina and open the fuckin door!..."

Any moment his father's relentlessness would
break down his mother...
her will,

     his mother.
  "yoli...
  yoli coño yoli! deja tu maldita mierda!...
  no me haga romper esta fucking baina...
  you know what i'll do!... ah? you know!"
  he took pause and breathed.
  "we don't gotta be like this mamita...
  come on, you know I love you. tu ta ahi?
  ah? are you listening? you're
  listening. i know it, i can feel you. come on
  negra you know i don't know how to be
  without you. ah?"
Another few minutes more and she'd let him in.
     that is why santa marta rejected her,
     a woman may choose to be weak,
     a mother may not!
But that is what a woman who loves like that
does, call it a syndrome if you want,

but it was predictable. Fucked up as it was,
it was love.

> *to her.*
> *to him.*
> *fuck knows why.*

The pole from the old Police-Lock slid to the
left and the chain came off the door. Leandro
came in, promising, as always, to be calm. They
spoke, exchanging words as the chain swung
and scraped to stillness. Sweet at first versus
her anger, his rage, then worse. Seconds
passed the first minute, maybe two, and he'd
grabbed her by her thinned lifeless mane,

> *she used to have such thick pretty*
> *hair, good hair like a blanquita you*
> *know, but not like dead flat, it like, it*
> *had curls... and not putting down*
> *nobody else's hair neither because*
> *people be thinking you trying to*
> *offend them and you not... you just*

like one freaking thing about
somebody. anyway it don't matter the
bastard was beating her ass,
twisting and tightening it to enforce his
domination. Pressing his lips against her ear,

"yo soy el hombre aquí coñazo... a mi se
me respeta!"

Stomping her resistance into silence brought
him a restrained contentment. Her eyes locked
on him, not frightened, but broken, like her.
His fists swinging like a money fighter with a
pinned opponent, he laid into her stomach and
face. Neither knew she was with child. It was
the second pregnancy since Juni. The last time
she had ended it with a few aspirin and a
German malta.
The pounding on her frail frame continued for
the longest minutes, she fought to free herself,
never in defense, she'd never raised her hand
to protect herself.

Panting, he paused only to catch breath and giggle on the exhale. She screamed, desperately hyperventilating, and coughing, until her voice no longer expelled. Neighbors, or rather those who resided in nearby apartments, sometimes called the cops, but NYPD rarely valued calls in this part of the city, and less in cases of domestic violence. Cries,

hers,

were eventually beaten, then beaten into intermittent moans of which only the half-dead are capable. Deaf to it, he dragged her limp body along the worn red carpeting passed Junito's open bedroom door like a caveman.

> *she'd been so happy when they'd gotten it. juni hated the cold of the tiles.*

He watched as they passed. The air would wrinkle each time. The child closed his eyes, *no,*

and covered his ears,

please,

no,

he screamed without sound. His vocal chords
strained. It was different tonight and somehow
it was worse. Trying to remember a happier
time he shook, clenching his teeth on the inner
rim of his bottom lip, his teeth glazing as the
blood mixed with the saliva, he remembered no
happy memories, only lesser pain. His mom's
anguish sent vibrations into his skin and Junito
absorbed them like a kitchen sponge.

that's probably why he had
asthma. doctor thought it was
emotionally induced.

He dumped her face down on the bed, she was
more gone than here,
Leo tugged at and pulled off his sweat-
drenched apparel. Her moaning aroused him. His
index finger and thumb stroked at her

neglected strands, he remembered it differently, maybe longer. Sliding off every article of her clothing, his lips gently touched her shoulders and down the welts along her spine. The single sided jabbing continued for hours, the mattress springs and frame were heard so clearly downstairs that la vecina,

> *that snotty cuerito with all*
> *them problem kids,*
> *banged her broomstick against*
> *her ceiling. maybe she should*
> *use it to clean her damn house.*

Leandro tensed and it ended. With almost a giggle under breath, he rolled off of her and slept, his wife shoved aside like a teen boy's sock.

His lungs strained from pushing his tears, Juni also slept until he awoke to a muted sorrow.

The apartment smelled of Leandro's musk,

weed and red label,
smothering like decomposing meat.

Drawn. He quietly wandered discovering his wet bruised mother trembling on the fire escape. Disoriented, divested, and dying. The marked and torn skin gave a horrid spotted appearance to her skin.
Frantically, he dashed to his bed and returned with his cartooned bed sheets,

raggedy ann and andy.

Juni covered her and held her until the Sun.

...THEN A BRITTLE AMEN

CHAPTER 4

Suddenly coherent, her lips swollen and quivering,

>her breath gasping,
>"that is not your father..."
>her inhale forced,
>and gurgling as the fluid
>flicked towards her uvula.
>"i swear... sska... ss... something
>went wrong... you'll know."

Juni listened,

>that's when it started, the hate,

cold tears dripped off his palms as they fell from her eyes and the warmth abandoned the body he embraced. He looked down at his hands, they turned callous and hard,

>a grown man's hands,

covered in clumping blood. Juni lifted her head,

>it was heavy,

and kissed her right cheek. It dropped back,
and away.

>"don't,
>
>please?
>
>don't leave me here,"

>>*could hear the wind rushin against his*
>>*ears, but didn't say nutin.*

Leandro slept,
unaware.
In the living room all that stood undisturbed
was a small jade dolphin pendant that Leo had
given Yoli when the baby was born.
Moments later, it dangled from Juni's neck as he
squeezed the rails behind him, his body at a
forty-five degree, his exhale stuttered, the
sidewalk calling to him, the impressions dug
deep into his fingers,

>>*could just let go,*
>>*it could all just stop,*
>>*he could make it just stop,*

but it did not that day,
it was not the time, not just yet.

When Yoli was buried, Juni tried to drop it into
her coffin before it closed, but his grip was too
tight.
He vomited,
his mommy's mother was embarrassed, then
angry.

...DANGLE

CHAPTER 5

The funeral came and went as did the trial.
Leandro was acquitted of murder, he pled guilty
to a drunk and disorderly. The prosecutor failed
to prove his guilt despite the physical evidence.
Leo claimed that an intruder likely entered the
home while he slept off a binge. Leo claimed no
recollection of the evening and even agreed to
and passed a lie detector test. No one wanted
to believe Leo, still without a witness it was
plausible, break-ins were up. The young
assistant district attorney could not convince a
jury that his guilt was beyond a reasonable
doubt.

The judge was seen crying after the case was
over and Leo was sent over to the Tombs,

> *the tombs is what everybody called*
> *the new york halls of justice and house*
> *of detention in the mid 1800's. the*
> *original egyptian mausoleum styled*

building is long gone but its'
replacement building kept the
moniker.

stevens would be proud i'm sure.

There he served another forty-two days. Junito
spent that time with his maternal grandparents
who took their pain and loss out on him.
Sometimes he'd be quietly playing,

matchbox cars or whatever,

and they'd rush up and backslap him,

"eres basura...
maldita sea la vida que la sangre de mi
hija corre por tus venas."

They'd knock over his food on the floor, they'd
step on or spit at it.
He lost weight quickly, often becoming dizzy,
and stumbling at times. Sometimes he'd vomit
so much bile that his throat, tongue, and lips
would strip raw. His grandmother wouldn't even

hold his head as he gurgled and choked, his hands and knees on the floor...

> *how a woman can make a child*
> *suffer like that.*

She'd dig her thumbnail in his ear until it was cleaned up satisfactorily.

Juni could only cry.

Leo's parents pretended as though their son had been erased, they would not consider taking in the boy, he had stopped existing for them also.

Once acquitted Leo was immediately granted custody of Juni who hadn't spoken since the incident. Truth is, Leo's release probably saved the child's life, the little man had developed pneumonia, he became anemic, his teeth were thinning, and his hair was falling out. The bruises along his back were, according to his grandmother, the result of clumsiness, as was his broken nose and perhaps the shard of broken fingernail embedded behind his infected earlobe. When they arrived home Leo sat his son down and told him that he did not understand or even remember the night's events. He admitted that unlike other times it tickled. As he spoke, he looked away uncomfortably, as he remembered, he looked back over at his son. His son stared,

one day you'll know.

...MAMA

CHAPTER 6

Things changed in the house after that,
Leandro's addictions intensified. He substituted
Yoli with an attractive mantequera named
Annie. The house became organized but filled
to capacity with stacked garbage bags stuffed
with clothing and cardboard boxes filled with
trinkets. It looked like a warehouse with red
carpeting and a kitchen.

Juni witnessed a more blatant and routine drug
presence in the apartment. Mounds of coke
were sifted on his mother's glass coffee table
and mixed with smaller mounds of cut,

> *el especial,*
> *it'll fuck you up all on its' own...*
> *or so they say.*
> *a little shop in the village*
> *created the blend.*

Annie could cook up base in the microwave,
which when done right would create air bubbles

in the process allowing for the illusion of greater volume,

> *marketing is important.*

It was more efficient than baby-jars, Leo still preferred to use a boiling pot and a wire hanger.

His thumbnail to the metal he'd slide the crystallization off the hanger. Juni would wrap a white handkerchief over his face and do tables. He would grab that straight razor, break down rocks, vial and put together a shift's bundles faster than two adults. Their vials were bigger than the competition's with their prismed three-dollar treys appearing the size of five-dollar nicks despite the same amount of material being used.

Junkies loved it.

> *manteca is tricky, you can only*
> *cut and bag-up what you needed*
> *for the day or two because it*
> *can react to the cut and go bad.*

quick.

At first the six-year-old was not allowed to work with dope or ether due to the sensitivity of the processes involving it, later on he became good at it. He cut down on the difficulty in measuring a dime-bag by using old Mick D's beverage stirrer spoons, one scrape off the top and you'd get a solid dime bag every time,

> *those little plastic shits were going for*
> *like a hundred a pop at one point.*

Later on, moldings of it were made in brass, gold and silver.

> *new spoons gotta be shaved if*
> *you don't got the cash.*

When he'd finished his chores early, Juni would sit in the living room and watch television. He enjoyed cartoons but was more a fan of news networks and science shows. Leo would buy books for him to read, but they were always books about some Dick and Jane, dogs, or stupid monkeys. They were silly and boring, Juni liked newspapers, they talked about everything and everyone.

The first afternoon after one day, Annie caught him reading a newspaper aloud. It was one of the local rag sheets she was using to wrap the countless figurines she'd shoplifted. She set aside a time for him to read to them. Leo avoided Juni, still he was ecstatic with the idea that his kid was speaking again. It made him feel like a father.

With Annie's encouragement Juni would come in the room and read to them. He could and would do so for long periods of time. Initially entertaining to the couple, that addiction-baked-in-nausea crept in. Their bodies achin' for bagged relief. Their sweat indicative of their bodies' inability to fight the need at last forcing Annie to reach for the ragged Dutch Master's box on the dresser. With only a shamed modicum of discretion, Annie would make her way under the sheets. There she would pull down Leo's pants and underwear and stroke his member tight until she found her grip, then slowly she injected his vein. Millions of sugar ants danced through her capillaries. The lighters' flame was again held to the spoon as it had only moments before. When right, when ready, the syringes' plunger drew back and sucked in that cure seasoned with traces of Leo. She'd then inject herself through one of the fat veins on her left foot,

> *not between the toes, i only*
> *seen that shit in movies.*

She never wore sandals back then. Sensually they'd touch, eventually going numb and fading into a dope-induced oblivion as Juni continued, undisturbed by the anesthetized bodies erotically embraced at arm's reach.

...ITCH

CHAPTER 7

Breakfast was overwhelming.

The three uncharacteristically walked down Broadway together in hopes that a speedy digestion would follow. As they passed one-o-first, Juni stopped and looked around, the couple waited. Leo grew increasingly aggravated.

                              "this is good
                              for a thing."

Over recent months Juni began asking questions. How things worked and why they were done in certain ways and not others, it irritated the living shit out of Leo, assuming the child's constant questioning to be babble.

"what is he talking about?"

        "i don't know leo. maybe if you talked to
        your son instead of at him you might

understand him."

"papi look!
we can see all around...
for like three blocks.
the projects ova theah, and, and,
and we on broadway.
we could put everybody in
theah."

"use your 'r's faufi, he's talking about a
spot leo."

Annie said as Leo took in his surroundings, for
the first time realizing that Columbus,
Amsterdam, and West End were all within
spitting distance.
It was like a corridor leading from the tecatos
to cash heavy weekend warriors. The entire
junkie spectrum, a customer for every time of
the day.
A month and one day later the spot was

cranking out two hundred plus bundles a day.
Didn't take long before New York's finest
caught wind of what was going on. The first
ones wanted their cut, and they got it...

after a little negotiating.
They'd give a heads up about upcoming hassles
and they'd earn a mortgage or car payment.
There was enough,

*all kinds of customers, always some
lonely someone singin' like they on
star search and whatnot,*
they formed long-ass lines around the corner
ensuring that remained the case. Fausto
learned a lot about people, watching those lines
from the lookout apartment across the street.
Moms, dads,
young girls, old men, bellies,
business-types, all colors, all creeds, all itchin'
all feenin',

*you almost wanna scratch from
under your skin,*

for la Bodeguita's relief. The control was
exciting, even at Fausto's age, actually more
so.
In they rolled,
Jersey, Connecticut plates,
blanquitos from college, party users. They
attracted attention.
When pitchin' dope you don't need but you
kinda hope for an O.D.

> *maybe two.*

Word spreads.

> *a good product speaks for itself.*

But an overdose mattered, the congressman's
son,

> *the supposed prodigy... remember*
> *watching him blow a dog once...*
> *can't remember why,*
> *he was so fucked up he probably*
> *wouldn't either.*

Anyway, unlike others, his death mattered, it

was bad,

> *just ask the press.*

They came kicking,

doors and dope fiends underfoot. Legal issues

mounted.

Used to be that payoffs were easy,

just a matter of leaving something in some

vieja's mailbox,

> *a few hundred in rent money.*

La Hara couldn't legally go in mailboxes with

them being under federal jurisdiction,

> *postal police... who you kiddin'?*

Cops would walk in after and grab their bit.

Then the Three-Fours dirty dozen got busted,

next the Two-Fours fuck-ups and everything

went to shit. The building became a target. An

easy bust they'd hit when city crime stats got

low.

> *...MOMS, DADS, YOUNG GIRLS, OLD MEN*

CHAPTER 8

Leo leaned his head against the chair behind the wall leading to the kitchen. He muttered as Juni happened by,

"we're going to have to close down one-o-first."

With his Chocodile still mostly in its' wrapper Juni pulled the piece away from his mouth and asked,

"why?

Irritated and surprised Leo grinded his teeth as he spoke.

"why? because the cops go in whenever the fuck they feel like it that's why? it's impossible to stay in business."

"then why don't we keep them out?"

Leo exhausted a sigh,

> "son!.. son... you'd need a fortress to
> keep them out."

Confused Juni asked,

> > "whatsa fortress?"

> "whoa... what's the fucking miracle
> you're not looking it up instead of asking
> me?"

Juni bit into his Chocodile, turned and walked
away.

> "yo... hey where you going?"

With a mouth full of the chocolate-coated
Twinkie Juni answered,

> > "to look it up."

> "no, wait, shit, relax, son hold on,
> comeback, i'll explain it to you. i'll tell you.
> uhmm remember when we went to dr.

and i told you about christopher columbus
discovering the island. remember? you
remember la fortaleza don't you?
remember he discovered all the indian
people."

Swallowing and shaking his head,

"i don't understand.
how you discover a place where
people already living? does
that mean if someone who
never been here before
comes in and finds my room
they can take it?"

Leo exhaled.

"nobody is gonna take your room juni.
columbus is not the point."

"then why you talking about him...
i don't understand papi."

"okay juni, do you remember that we

were inside this big-ass building, with really thick walls. i told you it was older than any other fort in this part of the world."

"yes."

"that was a fortress!"

"we have to have a building like that?"

"yeah something like that if we wanna keep all the cops out... we gotta find a new spot."

Juni chomped another bite and sat on the floor. His hands to his chin.

"ain't so easy right? don't you worry about it though... papi'll find something. it's just gonna take a lil time is all... we'll find a place you'll see, someplace we'll setup just for us. a place nobody gets in we don't want in."

                                "like beavers."

"beavers? no no fucking beavers, now what the fuck is you talking bout? it's a fucking building you can't get in... it protects from outside people who want to getchu, you can read a newspaper by yourself, how are you not getting this shit?!"

                        "we gotta be beavers."

"coño otra ve con lo beavers... que maldito beavers! why you keep talking about beavers?"

                                "cuz when I
                        watching tv yestahday
                        they was tawkin bout

  beavers

                        and that they make lodges."

        "so."

                                "so they be in theah"

"there!
pronounce your r's faufi!"

        "annie can you be quiet so i can figure out
        what the fuck he's trying to tell me! and
        close the bathroom door!"

"you don't gotta talk to me like that! you could
be nicer."

        "go ahead keep telling about the beaver
        hotel."

"always so damn rude!"

        "shut the fuck up!"

"i'm not gonna talk no more."

54

"okay! good!"

Then in unusual hop out and landing from the bathroom, Annie, her panties still at her ankles, exploded.
Slapping her thighs as she spoke.

"this is the problem with you leo. i work to correct him. to make sure he speaks right and you just ignore it. we're supposed to be a team to help him be better and you don't give a shit. i'm gonna take a shower don't talk to me."

"okay go ahead... beaver house."

"she's not done papi."

"what?"

As the shower droplets fell off her back and to the basin, her hands against the mustard yellow tiles, Annie breathed, inhaled, and screamed, "asshole!"

"does she call me that a lot?"

"everyday papi,
everyday."

"really" why?"

"really papi?"

"forget it whatever.
okay quick the beavers before she
starts again."

"so the big aminals...
amimals... an... anim...
animals! i got it!"

"yey, good finish the fucking story."

"the animals can't
get em.
why the building

can't be like that?"

Juni got up, shrugged, and walked off. Leo watched him go, placed his open palms over his face.

He grabbed and dialed the phone.

"mickey. your sister still

working at the wiz right? tell

her to rent me whatever they got

on beavers...

no not cartoons man, document...

document...

school and mutual of omaha type

video shit.

call her quick before

she gets pregnant again."

"fuck you leo."

...NORTH AMERICAN: CASTOR CANADENSIS

CHAPTER 9

Leo learned what a beaver lodge was and Spring came. The city started tearing up the asphalt in order to lay new gas pipe. Days later Leo put the word out, la Bodeguita was looking for construction equipment and supplies.

> *a junkie,*
>
> *pipero,*
>
> *tecato,*
>
> *can and will often pull off*
>
> *remarkable things if some dope*
>
> *is at the end of the rainbow.*

They brought cinderblocks, cement, steel gates, timber, and tools for every type of job. Rodney, a pipero and blackballed civil engineer was hired. The excess materials were dumped in the alley-sides in the back and side, which created a nasty, rust- ridden nightmare. Within weeks after the last bust the workers had sealed themselves in. The sub-ground access,

used to be an auto-parts back before, was a seventy-two-inch space on a razor-wire riddled eight-foot drop that ran around the street-sides, its' only entrance was thirty percent of a rebar exposed land bridge that met its' demise fairly early in the process.

Cops hit it but couldn't bust in through the steel and timber reinforced concrete with their Halligan tools, axes, and sledgehammers. Most precincts that needed them were on a waiting list to get use of one those new mobilized-battering-rams. People can tell you whatever they want, but Armored Rescue Vehicles (ARVs) were expensive and rare until way later. And when you've got a fuel crisis, a recession, and near empty city coffers, you ain't gonna be the asshole who stands up at a meeting and says let's take what little we got and buy pseudo-tanks that kick down doors.

When they got around to getting one to the spot it proved to be an embarrassment as the

unit's wrangler refused to chance the likelihood
of the vehicle falling in the gap and becoming
wedged. Lead officers agreed with him, after a
short career-based reflection.

They drilled into the walls, then came the
canisters of tear-gas which they inserted into
the sandbagged cavities between the walls.
Regardless, by the time they'd worked their way
passed a few inches everybody was gone.

The thing is most pipeline is buried one to two
meters deep. For a price and assuming that
bedrock wasn't an issue you could get someone
to dig deeper.

> *shiiit, they might even make it nice.*
> *money was money back then and it was*
> *worth it not to mess up your zodiacs*
> *making your way through a flooded*
> *tunnel.*

The cases against the workers fell apart since
the conspiracy to sell illicit drugs charges
became shaky after their two-star rats redacted

their statements,

        mothers and kids were then let go,
eventually most of the charges were
downgraded to trespassing and loitering, since
no one was actually caught in possession of any
drugs or drug paraphernalia. Plea-bargains and
adjournments in contemplation of dismissal were
dished out and one-o-first was again fully
staffed.
Rodney and his no longer needed services, sleep
soundly in the marshes off the highway near
LaGuardia airport.

...NEVER TO WAKE

CHAPTER 10

Time flowed in,

then on.

Juni was eight, he preferred to be called Fausti, his mother always called him Fausti. In second grade he excelled and was recommended for testing at the Niche School for Gifted Children. A place usually reserved for the children of the rich and disassociated. He tested at Annie's insistence and was rejected when he failed to match more than a couple of correct answers, they attributed it to guessing.

Annie demanded a review of the tests and threatened legal action. It was done and discovered that the child was mistakenly given the seventh grade level exam and his answers were being compared to third grade level answer sheet.

his actual score was a ninety-eight percent.

Fausti had also completed the four-hour exam early. School administrators wanted to place him several grades ahead, but Annie wouldn't allow it and decided one grade was enough. She refused to allow them to test his IQ.

Her angered voice, redolent of Paumonok,

"my faufi doesn't need you yuppie bitches to tell him he's smart, he's proven that and i won't let you tell him that there's some limit! we'll be back tomorrow... faufi grab your jacket."

"mrs. batista you have to underst"

"not married."

"i'm so sorry ok. miss?"

"nothing to be sorry about, mcgillicuddy."

"mcgillicudy?"

"no."

"wait what?"

"your question?"

"uhmm yes I'm
sorry what I was
saying...
uhmm what I was going to say
was, is, all children
are treated equally here at the
niche school."

"is that right?"

"absolute equality."

"eleven."

"i'm sorry, eleven?"

"the amount of years between 'all men are
created equal' and the 'three fifths
compromise'"

"i don't understand."

"i know sweetie, words are nice, have a

nice day. come on faufi."

The silenced dean waived goodbye and then requested that a desk be placed in the third grade classroom.

...MCGILLICUDDY

CHAPTER 11

A time then, when, way before much of this, Leandro had driven out to Valley Stream to make a delivery. As he exited the house, he came upon a young girl in a cheerleading outfit leaning on his car crying.

"what's wrong mamita?"

She moved away, her hair shifting and exposing a bloodied busted lip and bruised chin.
Jittering as she spoke,

"i'm sorry excuse me... sorry."

Leo caught up to and pressed her, persuading the young girl to talk. She turned out to be his customer's socially awkward little sister, a tall insecure adolescent with long reddish blonde hair that draped over her face.

pretty.

It took Leo about twenty minutes to get her to go have a meal with him. Leandro had just been acquitted on murder charges and he was surprised at how that did not seem to daunt her.

annabelle.

They spoke for hours,

about things.

Not always significant,

but things.

She wore a dizzy personality and was easily distracted, spewing random statements, but there was something that made Leandro trust her. The teen was honest, and he felt himself urged to believe in and help her.

There are some who will always tell you more than they should.

Her alcoholic mother had abandoned her and her brother Andy at a young age, since then he'd supported them. They were getting by as best they could then she reached the age of twelve, when, then,

her brother first began to touch her.

He beat her on her fourteenth birthday because when he raped her, he was unconvinced of her claims of virginity, since that time he would beat her whenever he felt she was not as he put it, tight.

Annabelle developed her love for dope from the neighbor boy. She confided in him to help her cope and he introduced her to it to help her cope. It only took her a few times to get hooked at which point he would only give it to her whenever she let him get on top of her. She was trying to wean herself off of it because the neighbor began protesting the condoms. She feared pregnancy or rather to what her brother might do to a baby and even kept a couple of 25mg DES in her sock drawer.

Leandro offered to handle Andy, but she wouldn't hear of it, instead he decided to return to the house, *to work something out.*

After a very brief negotiation he ended up
swapping an eight-ball of Fishscale for ownership
of the girl. Her brother accepted
without hesitation and Leandro drove off with
her towards the city.

"look you don't owe me nothing you
know, you can go anywhere you want... if
you need something just let me know.
there's a pen in the glove box, take down
my beeper."

her head hanging,

"i got nowhere to go,
maybe...
maybe i can crash with you
at your place till i like
figure something out you
know? like besides anyway i
understand that nobody ever

really gives nutin without
wanting something… so if
you want me to suck you off
or like let you fuck me i
mean whatever you don't
gotta feel bad. for real
you like helped me out a
lot so it's like alright I
mean it's you know… your
cool, you can. i'll do
whatever."

Leandro pulled over the red Pathfinder and
looked over at her.
He started the car and drove to Coney Island.
They spent that afternoon talking by the
teacups as night fell. Passed the boardwalk
Seagulls fought over trash as families washed
off the beach's opaque water. The two walked
on the beach eventually holding hands. The air
smelled of salt water and the sand and on their

feet was warm. Still, they continued speaking
until that awkward silence found its way in and
there were no few words.

"look i got my son,
if you want to watch him i will pay..."

In one motion Annabelle,

annie,

stopped walking and covered his lips with her
pinky finger,
smelled like berries.

"look leo i'm gettin tired,
my back hurts, my feet are
aching,
are we gonna like fuck or what?"

He kissed her and she pulled him against a
boardwalk support beam, their grunting

unconcerned with those who might have noticed. She'd been with boys before, and often, and she learned how to please them and get them to please her. Her teeth bit into his shoulder as he screamed the name of his dead wife. Annie didn't notice.

stupid kid.

He collapsed on her cheating her an instance before her sugarwalls would have tumbled. They laid there breathing on one another and whispering.

"how about I take care of
the both of you...
it sounds like your son
needs a woman in his life
as much as you do."

"HOW ABOUT YOU TWO GET DRESSED AND THEN GET THE FUCK OUTTA HERE BEFORE I CUFF YOU BOTH!"

The cop hollered as he stared down on them. The darkness concealed her face and clothing otherwise her age would have easily been apparent, and Leo would have surely gone back to jail. The officer walked away, maybe out of consideration, maybe to relieve himself, but allowing them the opportunity to get dressed and run to the car hand in hand, her undies featuring the happy hippopotami forgotten in the cooling sand.

The ride to the city seemed to go quickly. Annabelle hadn't stopped talking for more than the fractions of a moment she took catch her breath. At first Leo thought it was cute, all that energy, all that

excitement. Then she went on, and on, all that energy, all that excitement.

keep driving.

Leo muttered, his lips barely moving, then, shaking his head no as his finger flicked off the turn signal he was about to use to pull over and kick her out.

His temples thumping, they arrived at the
building an hour later,

"annabelle this is my son fausto, we call
him juni, juni this is annabelle."

Leaning over to his height she spoke to him in a
nearly animated voice,

"hi faufi, you don't
mind if i call you
faufi do you? you can
like call me annie if
you want."

Juni stared blankly, at nothing, then at her,
unresponsive and uninterested in her
attempts, and her. In the coming days and
weeks, she bought him toys and made silly
jokes, nothing worked. Annie became so
frustrated at times that she often cried

hysterically in the bathroom eventually
embracing more heroin to bring her down and
help her forget her memories and failures. Time
trickled and Annie's addiction continued making
her more and more neurotic and quirky. One
night similar to most she tucked Juni into bed
and watched him as he lay in bed not sleeping.
She could feel his sadness in her chest, and she
kneeled in front of his bed.

"once, way back and
long ago, in a time
when giants were all
the earth knew. there
was a tiny worm that
glowed bright as it
moved through the
rainforest. back then
the world was dark, i
mean like completely
black when the sun

went down. nothing in the sky. when the worm wandered, the animals could see, they found food, much more food than in the day and it was a lot less dangerous for the smaller animals you know because like not as many of the big animals were awake. anyways, this tiny worm would only glow for three hours. that's it. nothing more. now most of the animals were ok with that, i mean it was better than before. but a little monkey,

not much bigger than
a cat, decided to one
day walk up to this
tiny glowing worm and he
tells her,
'hey you, tiny glow worm, why
don't you glow for longer. why
can't you give us more time?'
'sorry monkey, i must sleep in
the sun and soak it up all day
so that i can glow at night. i
wish i could do more.'
well, the monkey put
its' knuckles under
its' chin and thought...
and thought... and
thought some more.
suddenly, he jumped
up all excited and
ran until found the
glow worm.

'i think i know a way! i'll find
you here tomorrow.'

the next day when the
sun went down and the
darkness took its'
hold the monkey put
its' hand out. the
excited glow worm
climbed on. without
warning he shoved her
in his mouth. she was
so frightened she
curled up into a ball
as he swirled the
tiny worm in his
mouth. running then
climbing from tree to
tree until he reached
the tallest one.
staring straight up
into the black sky,

the little monkey
grabbed a straw he
had behind his ear,
put it to his lips
and spit the worm
high into the air. as
she rose she found
herself floating and
cold. she could see
the sun in the
distance but she
would never again
come home. the glow
worm began to weep,
as she wiped her
tears and the
droplets sprinkled
the sky.
she's still up there.
sometimes she's
balled up.

sometimes she
stretches forming
crescents or half
circles.
as the time of giants
passed and people
took their place.
everyone forgot about
the worm. eventually
they named the light
in the sky moon and
her tears stars.
never knowing to
thank her."

"that's a terrible story lady."

Annie smirked,

"maybe it is.
listen baby boy...
i... i can't make it better

faufi,

but i promise to be here

for you if you need me.

when you need me."

Juni looked up at her stretched up his head pressing and holding his lips to her cheek, her hand in his. Annie blushed and stayed there watching him until he at last slept, then she laid her head and listened to his heartbeat. It was at that moment that she knew she couldn't avoid loving him, a hollow space in her life filled and for the first time in a long time she tasted happiness. Leandro looked at them from the doorway, he did not love her, and he knew he never could,

still loves her,

but he felt like Juni needed her and that she needed Juni. Quietly he walked away, something telling him he did something right.

...HE STILL LOVES HER

CHAPTER 12

The infant girl's eyes followed the orisha as she
lingered near the foot of the hospital bed. Her
concerns only multiplied as she listened to the
test results. For months she had entered the
belly in hopes of influencing but was unheard.

...SHE'S WATCHING

CHAPTER 13

It was brick outside, he was alone,

again,

looking out from the old Astrovan's passenger
seat. Some of the girls were pretty, a few only
slightly older than him. The green thermos was
ugly and huge,

mmm... chocolate,

he sipped slowly to keep from scorching his lips
as the junkies lined up.

As spots go, one-o-eight Manhattan Ave. was a
lot hotter than one-o-first. In an hour or two
cops would charge in, and material would be
dropped into the flaming garbage cans that
served as heaters. Bundles were wrapped around
an Rx vial full of charcoal lighter fluid in order to
stay ahead of the cops because cops were
getting better. Plus, that fucking Charlie
Chopper, he'd killed five people in the
neighborhood and hadn't been caught. The

patterned murders were bringing a ton of attention to the area and the cops couldn't track him. Had he and his victims been anything other than Latino, the press and FBI would have rightfully labeled him a serial killer.

> *can't waste on a population that don't*
> *vote and don't wanna speak no english.*

Fausti was studying the process and surroundings. He shuffled his feet in frustration careful to not kick the little revolver nestled under the mat.

There was a knock at the glass. He rolled it down.

"i know who you are."

She was pretty, with dark, dead straight hair,
> *like a china's.*

Her glasses were thin rimmed and slowly making their way down her nose.

"can I sit with you?... it's really cold
out here."

Pushing the piece completely under the mat, he
let her in.

"my moms is coppin by the way, that line
looks it's gonna be a while. wait is that
hot chocolate? ooh can I have a sip?"

Handing her his cup she sipped, savoring it like it
was everything, as he sat quietly and listened,
she talked, a lot, like Annie, but fun stuff. He
was shy, but the ritual soon came daily. They
grew close, talking as children can, making the
time go.

Her name was Serena.

...DOPE AND HOT COCOA

CHAPTER 14

Serena made no secret that she liked him, she told Fausti about girls, what they liked, how to kiss, what she'd learned to like.

Annie erupted when she found out, becoming aware of the activity when she accidently walked in on Fausti fighting tears in an effort to pee through the swelled burning sensation and discharge.

Heart-broken.

Mortified.

Pissed.

She backhanded him, hugged him then backhanded him again. Immediately bringing to light the how's and who's.

Her nails clamped into his forearm she yanked him into a cab to go find Serena, she got hit too...

little puta!

She took them both for medical treatment,

examinations, and blood tests. They continued their relationship after that with Fausti supplementing her mother's income and habit so that Serena wouldn't have to whore for her mommy's dope money.

...BURNING YOUNG LOVE

CHAPTER 15

"The instinct to command others,
in its primitive essence,
is a carnivorous, altogether bestial and
savage instinct."

Mikhail Aleksandrovich Bakunin

It was an unusual situation, but the air Fausti
carried was not like that of anything usual.
Juni's, AKA Fausti's, AKA Faufi's, full name was
actually Fausto Leandro Batista Jr., over time Jr.
fell off.
At nine he took an interest in what his father
referred to as

la cuestion

and he referred to as the

la bodeguita

after the corner grocery store owner talked to
him about the pride of ownership and nothing in
life being better than owning your own little

Bodeguita. Leo began consulting Fausti, taking less action unless his son agreed with it in an effort to groom him for eventual takeover.

By simply being in Fausti's company you just felt assured and safe, questioning the child felt unnatural. That and also that there were people, useful people, who seemed to be drawn to them. People like Peres Peron, a Chilean investment banker and an old customer of Leo's. Peron would attach six figure amounts or less as riders to legitimate wire transactions using concentration or suspension accounts. Banks commingle funds from different sources later sorting for wire transfer in large washes or sweep accounts. During the sorting, the riders, *for which there was no paperwork*, would be plucked and merged into larger amounts, at which point loans would be directly deposited by further institutions into series seven type commercial investment accounts. These accounts often slid into superfunds, which are obese even less regulated hedge funds. It seems like a lot but a few zeros a month in something like that is easy to hide. Eventually everybody you know has one of your businesses in their name. And you'll be able to trust those individuals so long as you hang something over them. Cash and guns aren't enough. They need the fear of traumatizing life alteration compelling them to stay in line. It doesn't matter who, or how they're connected to you. Those are the rules, that's how it works, it's the only way it can.

> *otherwise, a couple of years*
> *locked-up and you'll come out*
> *penny-less.*

Indirectly, La Bodeguita purchased the first of several laundromats, arcades, and other cash-based businesses with the help of another, a disgraced lawyer named Norton Beal.

Beal was disbarred when he broke the attorney client privilege and announced to the media that his client was indeed a child molester thereby destroying his client's career in early childhood psychological research and education. Peron found him after the media frenzy stopped and his book and movie deal fell through when his client committed suicide by setting himself on fire while screaming of his innocence.

Beal was labeled a liar and was being sued until at closed hearings he played a taped excerpt of his client,

> "boys like that, they don't know what
> they are yet, all i do is take em to a place
> they maybe would've found eventually."

The civil case was dropped but his reputation and career were ruined. The family later purchased the tapes for a substantial yet undisclosed amount of money, their contents have never been made public.

Still, Beal was an excellent attorney, he was exceedingly intelligent and very private about his personal life. No one really knew anything more than what was released to the media and that was limited. One time, Fausti questioned the action that cost him his career.

"someday you'll get it."

Regardless, Fausti adored him. Beal watched over him and pushed him to better himself, always making it a point to expose him to those things which would most stimulate his hunger for understanding.

"you were born to be more than just a drug pusher, fausto."

Smiling Fausto would not respond,

when they stop wanting it we'll stop selling it.

He'd then wink and go on doing whatever he was doing.

...SOMEDAY

CHAPTER 16

Charming like a single-breasted prostitute, Leo fused relationships with the Rossiyas and Tian Di Hui societies. Both the Cundinamarcas and the Atzlans would invite him to family events.

> *men bond over coke,*
>
> *they just do.*

It was no secret Leo could party, he could draw anyone into his circle, smoke a doobie, do a bump, and make a memory.

Fausti too had made some friends.

His role, however, was not always behind the scenes. Most however, assumed at his fathers' direction. One occasion comes to mind when he was maybe twelve, he decided to send a message to Flaco-Chichi, someone too big to be a competitor. Flaco-Chichi was nicknamed that because he was very thin and visited his mother religiously. He was a well-established icon on the streets. He could move a couple dozen or so kilos a month just locally.

Also.

Moving only a brick or two at a time. Flaco steadily trafficked shipments in and through New York, PA, and Ohio. He built up this block to be a haven for his mother and if someone wanted him gone, they'd have to remove him. A couple of years back some cops tried to make a push, but word got out that other people's money would be affected, and they were quickly reassigned.

On a late morning while waiting at the counter for the bakery to pull a tray from the oven, a child handed him a Startac and ran away. It rang, and the voice on the on the other end gave him until ten that night to retire. He laughed, flipped it shut, and dropped it in the trash and Doña Mercedes handed him his mother's loaves.

> "mandale un besito a tu mai,
>
> y oye chichi,
>
> portate bien mijito okay, teng cuidado."

She'd been sending his mom her love and telling him to behave all his life, there was no reason for today to be any different.

The night zipped along nicely.

He placed some extra workers out and hung on his mother's stoop in case something stirred.

10pm

nothing.

A couple of kids were still playing off the curb with some chiming Barbie knockoff on a red mechanized bicycle that peddled in circles.

Flaco was anxious. Shit had a habit of getting fucked quick.

A minute later an old work van rolling down the block suddenly jumped the curb and bashed into the trash day's ashcans.

The cinders clouded everything.

Pistols blazed as the passengers leaped and pumped shots into everything. Most were so busy reacting that they didn't notice the other cargo vans racing across from either side of the block.

Fausti shouted orders as he leaped last from one of the vehicles and gunned down two guys who were too stunned to reach or run.

Nobody knew where to go; it was impossible to steady a shot. Quintana and Yaya sprayed the tenement windows with clip after clip to keep the nosey tucked away and any cover fire at bay. Nearby, another young one with no sense fell facedown, his teeth scraping against the concrete.

A projectile came so close to Fausti that it blew apart his azebache, grazing the skin.

> *it's a shiny little black fist made from fossilized jurassic era trees in case you're wondering... you know good ole dominican juju.*

He'd worn it on his wrist since birth,

> *burned...*

> *distracted.*

The butt of a revolver slammed into his temple,

everything squiggled as Fausto slammed into the ground, his index finger snapping backwards and his palm's edge sliding along the concrete, embedding skin and blood. Flaco's boot stomped on Fausto's wrist, releasing his already loosed grip on the pistol. Dropping down on him so that his bleeding hand, waist, and hip were pinned, Flaco pushed down his hand's hold on Fausto neck against the pavement and dropped fist after fist on him. Fausti forced a cough to clear the blood from his throat flowing down his nasal passages. He was big and strong for a kid his age, but Flaco was a man,

he'd come up on the streets. Flaco was out of bullets and wasn't about to let go of this kid to go find some.

He heard shots, running and fighting, he knew at least some of his men were alive, once he got rid of this,

this little fuckshit,

he'd regroup and get things back under control.

Fausti swung his free arm trying to block the blows and push him off,

> *getting harder to understand what's going on... getting darker.*

Teeth clenched,

"if i had one more motherfucking bullet this would be over."

Fausti's arm was barely moving anymore. His eye was swelling shut as he watched Flaco pick up and wrap both hands around his revolver, aim at his head, and arch back. He could feel the air dividing as it was coming down as his eye swelled completely shut,

> *it would be quick.*

He flopped to the asphalt, then nothing.

Shots.

Shots.

Then silence.

The weight came off, he was floating.

> *too much light, then none.*

An engine started and he was placed down, a door closed.

In less than ten minutes, the bodies were everywhere, bystander and opposition alike, blood flowing through the cracks soaking into the blackened bubblegum that had fused to it. As Fausti's van pulled away, the old mother who Flaco adored, stepped out of the building, looked upon her dead son, pressed her clenched her fists to her chest, and stopped living, never releasing. The emptier vans crossed the George Washington Bridge moments before the Police ESU arrived.

Nobody noticed Serena watching behind the garbage bags covering the walk-down under the cleaners. She'd watched Quintana run up and drop a bullet in Flaco-Chichi's head, she'd seen everything, and her belly grew cold even under all she wore to conceal it. Her dead mother still kneeled at the base of the stairs, folded cash still in hand as was the gentleman they were pleasuring,

mom and daughter worth more.

Serena went through their pockets, stuffed her
pockets, and ran, hard.

The Barbie knockoff continued chiming and
peddling in circles.

After, the bodies were removed and the law
gone, the superintendents came from their
subterranean residences and washed the drying
red,

much red,

from the concrete. The weighted attar of blood
endured for days and like all things it all was
eventually forgotten with the rain.

The day next, when he arrived from Jersey, he
was bandaged heavily. Annie nearly had a stroke
when she saw him. Immediately, she cut the
gauze and tape and placed him in the tub, after,
she forced a couple of Tylenol III's into his
mouth, bandaged him up and put him to bed. He
slept for days.

leo was pissed.

When the swelling went down and he finally rose from bed Beal was in the living room.

"you little shit!
you could have been killed.
you have a lot of
blood on your hands...
was it worth it?"

Fausti looked at Beal as surprised as he was disappointed by the comment.

"it needed to happen.
next time i'll be more careful."

Sorrowfully, Beal looked at the boy,

"fausti,
how in the hell can
you be okay with what you
did?"

"you don't live in my skin... don't try."

...HEAVY IS THE BLOOD

CHAPTER 17

"I kill without compunction and remember all my killings.
Treason must be scotched by fair means or foul before it overwhelms me.
The oaktrees of insurrection grow from the acorn of treachery."

King Hydrota

Annie woke him with an All-American birthday cheer, a tradition she began three years prior when she became sober. She hadn't done drugs in about thirty-seven months, three days, and seven hours,

> *give or take a minute and an*
> *occasional joint,*
> *but weed don't really count.*

Everyone discovered that under that junkie exterior she was an obsessive compulsive with a good heart and way too much energy. She was there a woman, in her early- twenties, in a green and yellow cheerleader outfit,

the same one leo had "met" her in,

leaping and singing happy birthday. She hugged him, kissed his forehead, and went off to clean and cook. The house changed with her, everything in the home was white under the direction of the new Annie who donated all of her thieved trinkets and junk to the homeless,

that'll feed em!

She'd gotten her GED.

Leo had sworn off coke, he blamed it for the death of Yoli,

his yoli.

He still needed a little dope before bed in order to sleep, but that was different. To the surprise of some, a Manteca user can actually function quite well for quite a while as long as his fix is consistent,

still dependence will eventually
force imbalance.

The times came when Leo would have lost everything if it hadn't been for Norton's coaxing. With his flaky personality and his lack of reliability it was only a matter of time before things came crashing down like a supermarket tower of olive jars. Fausto could not look at him without hearing a resounding scratching in the back of his head. Leo became something resembling a father, but Fausto's pain lived deep.

On hot days one could see people hanging out on the winding fire escapes to avoid the unbearable heat indoors. An air conditioner can slap some serious fat onto a Con-Ed bill and when rent takes two thirds of your family's income, a cooled room exposes itself as a luxury. But this birthday the day was not so hot. Fausto sat on the fire escape staring at the dust particles in the Sun, nodding without blinking or speaking. He seemed to be listening, for something, for someone.

a sign...

any sign

The little gordita from the red brick building across the street was blowing him kisses in her bright yellow communion dress, he didn't see her. A couple of clankers landed nearby,

nasty-ass rat birds,

scavenging for anything edible.

He'd sat on that fire escape every birthday since his mother died, this year however, there was a rather brutal intensity in the air, it was furious, smelling of burnt nutmeg. Wispy clouds knotted above, they were ordered to gather and shield the soon mourning Sun from what was to occur. Fausti climbed in through the living-room window and tossed a crushed candle on the table, he was perspiring in globs. Leandro staggered out of the bedroom looked at his son whacked him on the shoulder and muttered something ending in birthday.

Later that day, Fausto met up with his father at

the Ureña Grocery over on Columbus Ave., they hopped in a Pathfinder and drove off followed by a second vehicle with protection. They parked in the park near the Cloisters in uptown where business was discussed. The type of place where cops took cuffed hookers at night to plead and take sentencing.

At the time it was widely and wrongly believed that the surrounding power lines along with loud music interfered with police eavesdropping equipment. The other car's music wailed. Leo was talking about how to keep the workers from skimming the shake off incoming bricks.

> richard loshbough and edward pryor were the first to request a patent for their digital scale in 1980, they weren't immediately assimilated into use. accuracy and reliability weren't immediate, they required skills and constant calibration and were very much a specialty item. it was a while

before most were doing more than
five six hundred grams at a time on
readily available triple beams. when
kilos land they are usually over the
2.2lbs, the surplus commonly known
as shake is often trimmed by workers,
before it gets stepped on, in order to
maintain consistency during the
cutting process.

Workers tend to, more often than not, keep that little amount for either personal use or a quick side sale. It is usually overlooked because of the minimal amount and its non-effect on the bottom-line, but when you're moving dozens upon dozens of bricks, a few grams a kilo adds up to major opportunity costs and actual competition from within. Leo wanted Fausto to put together a way to control it.

"i'll get on it."

Leo pulled a menthol from his pack and lit it. With the cigarette hanging of his lip,

"papi i know i been a shitty dad to you,
but i love you...
and...
and i know it don't make no sense, but i
loved your mother. i miss her every day.
you know?"
Looking piercingly into his father's eyes,
  brown like his, but moist.
And then there were shots.

...GORDITAS AND GUNSHOTS

CHAPTER 18

Leo squealed as he covered his crotch in a fruitless effort to push the gushing blood back into his body,

his son leaned towards him.

> "these are the last
>
> seconds pop...
>
> don't remember nothing but
>
> her,
>
> just her."

There was a pause,

momentary at best, but it seemed longer.

> *a breath.*
>
> *then.*

Leaning back, he placed two more through his father's temple, ending him.

Without hesitation he hopped out and opened fire on the other vehicle killing its' passengers.

Their deaths were probably not necessary, but they who are dead can't snitch.

Quickly he took the lighter off his father's body and set both vehicles ablaze. Fausto wiped and tossed the emptied snub nose onto the burning seats whose crackling consumed the sound from the system. He made it all the way to Broadway before the first explosion. There he caught a gypsy cab.

> *can feel it pushing through my*
> *pores,*
> *rage,*
> *just empty,*
> *the loss,*
> *all of it,*
> *feel it,*
> *the void,*
> *the nothing.*
> *want release,*
> *then,*
> *nothing.*

The driver smelled of thieves' oil and damp cloth. Fausto aggressively rubbed his hands over his forearms until the wax flaked off. Discretely he brushed it off the seat and his clothing. Finally arriving at his destination, he went swimming at the public pool for the rest of the day.

The flames burned, Fausto swam, the clouds were dismissed, and the Sun was again freed, to see.

News of the deaths came the next day. Fausto identified the charred remains of his father and Annie incessantly wept for days. He comforted her as best he could, it was difficult. The police did not question him. They assumed it was a professional.

The first three bullets in the weapon were loaded with mercury ensuring the death of his father, and the others were magnesium tipped causing incendiary damage to whatever they hit.

The fire department arrived and quickly realized that the abundance of open johnnypumps around the neighboring areas caused a dramatic loss in water pressure. The flames were allowed to burn out. Nothing put him at the scene and no authorities suspected.

At fourteen Fausto now had to prove his worth, he would have to become what his father seemed to be. He consulted Beal who he told of a plan,

ninety days,

Beal snickered and shook his head.

The night before everything was to begin Fausto, at Beal's insistence, consulted a local Esperitista named Margaro Osmín who while possessed by one of the Seres,

demigods,

spoke to him.

He was a chubby somewhat soft gestured man who wore bright colored garments and spoke with a lisp. The room was dark lit only by five candles, there were smells of incense and tobacco. All the walls were dingy from the decades of candle flame, on them were light

bleached images of saints. On the tables there
were more saints, statues of various sizes. The
table supported a huge clear gauntlet filled with
water; a crystal sat inside of it.
With his eyes rolling back he spoke in an old
rough whispered tone,

> "you will have opportunities to fix
> your life, all actions are connected...
> see your surroundings and what
> follows.
> mijo tragedy sleeps warm under your
> tongue,
> those you have felt,
> those you cause.
> you can walk away, now, someday then.
> you will feel her suffering when you
> fail to do so.
> you will hear her joy if you do.
> still,
> you are unconscious of purpose, and

nothing,

nothing can stand without

understanding.

come, but only when i send for you...

never before.

que Dios te bendige siempre mijo."

...FLAKES

118

CHAPTER 19

Margaro Osmín was born and burdened early in life with a limited something. Something that allowed him to heal by briefly becoming ill. Though it never felt brief to him. Daily agony and discomfort.

> *always vomiting, sweating,*
> *coughing, aching, his limbs*
> *would fold. there was so much*
> *screaming. usually at night*

By the age of five he'd cured hundreds.

On his sixth birthday Margaro Osmín was playing with other children under the day's Sun. America was at war in the Dominican in order to ensure peace. Pockets of gunfire broke out often. The mother and son lived near Ciudad Nueva and stray bullets often whizzed by and through houses of those in the surrounding areas, one entered through the home and out the front door directly into Margaro Osmin's chest as he played outside, sending him down like a forty-pound death punch to the ground.

Concomitantly, miles away in Haiti, one of the most powerful brujas the island ever produced died of a broken heart. The spirit worlds screamed for a cease-fire,

guns jammed,

and those within walking distance came to see the dead boy of the miracles. The crowd watched as the hysterical mother squeezed and rocked her son.

Like vapor from warm bread a tall man in a white linen suit and hat emerged from the crowd. He forcibly released the child's body from his mother's grasp and began to operate. Everyone looked on as the tall man in the white suit and a hat inserted his fingers in the chest cavity, sewed the stitches, stood, stepped over the little corpse, and then walked into the crowd as inexplicably as he had come from it. No one recalled his face. Margaro sat-up, his stomach

was growling with hunger. The bullet dangling
from a string about his neck.
No longer able to heal, he resurrected with the
gifts of the dead bruja plus,

> *se montaba,*

he would become possessed by any one of the
numerous Orishas at will. Margaro Osmin gained
the ability to commit endless acts of wonder but
was voided any ability to cause harm. The old
bruja was found days later in an isolated tin
roofed shack outside Saint Pietre. She was in her
rocker bloated with the tattered photo of a boy
gripped to her chest,
it smelled of sadness in that little red shanty,
longing, not death.

...VAPOR

CHAPTER 20

96th street, passed the Hudson River drive to the benches that overlooked the river. Where Yoli would take him when she needed to think. Where he went now. They stood looking out over the river.

"why'd you kill him?"

Beal's question spiked.

"what would make you think i could..."

His finger unapologetically pointing,

"cut the shit! i know you. i know it wasn't about greed. i'm assuming it was about your mother... i'll drop it for now, but i eventually want an answer from you boy. remember i know you."

Beal walked off silently.

another day.

...WHY

CHAPTER 21

Leo's charred corpse was 48 hours cold when the first of La Bodeguita's workers was found tortured in a Broome Street basement across from the dumpling place. Workers took off with cash and product. Penny hustlers at best, young cats with hard-ons for flash and the always orally munificent chicken heads,

not always female.

Many reckoned that with the boss dead they could lay claim to the spots.

Other than the fourteen-year-old son of a dead man, Fausto was no one.

Sicanis wanted more now. With the Feds and the Fis eating away at their influence, from a cash hungry point of view it was either about shitting or getting off the pot. It was always a delicate balance with them. The Sicani mob is full of traditions and reputations. In contrast with the hood, which is full of unpredictable hormonal teens that only want their bellies and wallets full,

*hard to fight anything when you don't
ever know where it's coming from.*

He'd acted early.

A sleepless week in hiding later, Fausto managed to come home. With a throated exhale, he slid under the sheets. As he shifted something poked through the pillow. Quickly he shook the case only to have a Betamax and some hair strands fall from it. Inspecting it first, he got up and played it.

A few flickering screens of static then his front door came into view. First outside, then inside, it glided through the apartment and to Annie's room. There the filmer's slender fingers extended over her body. Tracing her form for several seconds with a razor, slowly slicing the threads of her fitted nightshirt, then it turned to static. He exploded violently, finding himself little more than severely frustrated shortly thereafter.

Despite a radiant Sun, it rained Saturday. A witch from the Upper East Side married her lover that morning. Annie stayed home cleaning. She noticed an opened box of blue laundry dye near the garbage chute as she tossed out a half dead fern.

As if she'd expected it to be there Annie picked it up and walked in and to the bathroom. There she stripped her clothes, mixed the indigo powder with hand lotion in the vanity's basin. When thick she dipped her fingers and rubbed her skin.

Annie was normal when she did all things done, because to her all things were normal. Fausto continued to take care of her because she was of the good and he loved her. He never, however, spoke of business in front of her. Even when Beal visited.

Paranoia seeped through every pore as everyone morphed into enemies. He began driving different cars every three or four days as a precaution.

Beal noticed a ratty Tech 9 and a pair of magazines on the shelf over the door between the plastic sleeved image of St. Michael spearing the devil and the cup of coffee.

"fausto, your father is dead a month. you can let this die too, you have money. time to live.

leave everything and move down to the island with my fam... with me?

i can teach you to be a kid, and let you be one. for the first time you'll be able to breathe."

arm on shoulder

"you'll never have to look back."

Fausto's head fell from the weight of the offer, he was tired, and he wanted out. He was personally responsible for much death. Suddenly there was a possibility of starting over. Of erasing the bad.

"what the hell happened to the vcr?"

it lay smashed in the corner of living room.

Fausto's rage returned, more bitter, leaving a taste in his mouth much like bile only metallic. Beal reluctantly didn't push...

discussion over.

...NOW ON BETA

CHAPTER 22

*if you don't have volume distribution,
weight, you will always be at the mercy of
the distributor leaving you powerless over
quality, pricing, and availability. thus,
making you a gang or a crew to be
manipulated and sacrificed at will.*

The Cundinamarcas were for the moment the go
to distributors when it came to coke. They
produced Manteca too, but Cundi-White lacked
the kick the Asian dope had, but in all fairness,
they were also new to the processing and
cultivating of the poppy and in a few decades
things might likely be different.

...IT'S DOPE

CHAPTER 23

Medellin got outsmarted by Cali, Mexico was hungrier than South America, Panama got too smart for the United States and had to be caged with no voice for song. Ball's ain't never enough.

A war exhausts a shitload of resources. Thus, making a move on La Bodeguita unwise if it managed to ride the fence throughout the ordeal. Profits would grow if they could remain a reliable distribution point. Usually during war when so much blood is spilled, that people tend to hold on to what they have rather than venture into new areas or headaches. La Bodeguita would have to make war costly to keep their hold and get Fausto acknowledged. Sunday morning, Edmonds placed an incendiary device juxtaposed to the gas tank of the car that Libi Pinzon would be driving that day. A cool morning's dew forced him to adjust several times for moisture. The explosive device was rigged to explode when she chirped the car alarm.

It failed.

At half-passed noon Libi was at Woodberry Commons shopping. As she walked away from her car with her gaggle of friends, she realized she'd forgotten her keys. It would be a moment that Malenia handed Libi her bag trotted to the car her heels clacking.

She'd leaned in through the driver side window that Libi had forgotten to roll up. Her fitted skirt slid cleanly up her thighs to the delight of the sweaty teen assigned to collect carts in that parking lot.

Hooking the key ring with her index finger she lifted them and twirled around in triumph as the car alarm automatically locked the door and a sudden massive explosion shot from beneath the vehicle lifting it. Libi screamed as Malenia's

hips and torso launched out like a flaming
projectile that knocked her down, broke two ribs,
and singed her eyebrows.

Nestor Pinzon was enraged.

almost lost her.

He called Malenia's parents and with weighted
tongue listened to the mother,

inconsolable.

She had been Libi's best friend since they were
toddlers, another daughter really. One hour later
Antonio Fernandez, leader of the powerhouse
Atzlan, was butchered and his entrails forced
fed to his family, all their hangouts were
bombed, and war ensued. Atzlan out of Juarez
had a long history.

Their heritage could be traced all the way back
one way or another to when desperados
saturated Mexico and Western America,

or when western america was
mexico.

They fit the bill since they'd caused so much

tension by taking so much market share from the Cundinamarcas.

Retaliation, began with the kidnapping,

from her hospital bed,

and defiling of Libi Pinzon. She was found impaled, her face nearly coated, on a gently swinging wrought iron alley door.

Atzlan went after Pinzon, killing two more of his children and a dozen or so of his men. Stash houses were set ablaze in turn saw more of their own killed.

A fortnight later, a small, chilled gift box addressed to him arrived by express mail at one of his restaurants in Corona Queens.

The note attached said,

"you have your daughter's eyes."

When he finally opened it, he frenziedly wept as he stared upon them.

To the Tian Di Hui, entering a war was both unprofitable and unnecessary since their product

was dope not coke. They viewed La Bodeguita as an entity and did not care who led it as long as it did what it was supposed to. They adjusted their distribution agreement. They demanded a significant increase on orders and,

on consignment of course,

reluctantly converting La Bodeguita into an entry-level wholesaler.

The increase was substantial, and the Chinese mob was not tolerant of late payments. La Bodeguita began dipping into profits in order to keep face. Fausto did not have the demand to move that much product. Beal called on the assistance of an old buddy of Edmond's in Coney Island, a swarthy Pakhan named Vaclav Skolka. Skolka was a Ukranian ex-Colonel who ran an entire sect of the Bratva operation out of a Brooklyn retirement facility. Beal handled negotiations because he would have likely killed Fausto had he believed him really in charge and often complemented Beal on being brilliant enough to place a boy as a front- man. They sold to him for several points under market value with the relationship tone that it was more of a partnership agreement rather than a buyer seller deal. In time Fausto's involvement in dope became profitable, but never lucrative, better than his father's, but less stable. By default, La Bodeguita was less of a target due to apprehension of a messy conflict with the Rossiyas. In the past the Sicanis feared few, but an organization made up of former Soviet soldiers and KGB was formidable.

especially with the gq don dead.
Streets got barbaric, La Bodeguita, more strengthened, was becoming a liability to itself. The war reached its' thirteenth month, and the death toll was high, as were the disappearances. The federal government was putting together a special task force to bring down the factions. The actual removal of Pinzon and or Atzlan would cause Fausto's activities to fall squarely

under a microscope and send La Bodeguita into
a new wave of headaches.

> it comes down to a willingness to do
> what is needed. anybody can kill and
> fuck what you heard and who said it,
> the reactions are but three; disgust,
> arousal, or indifference. you can
> usually tell who feels what by what he
> or she does after.
> street shit is just nasty, always has
> been, and the wrong
> people get hurt, assets are wasted at
> explosive rates, and the outcome,
> though always more sympathetic for
> one side while still not necessarily truly
> favorable.
> often wars are ended by very different
> people than those who start them.
> there is only so much you can handle,
> when enough people have watched
> enough people die it ends... with

losses, replaced leaders, handshakes,

and money.

Fausto survived.

...WORKING IT OUT

CHAPTER 24

The other Batista's, parents of Leo, were a rather handsome couple from San Jose de Las Matas. He, Fausto Manuel Batista, was the son of a young priest who had abandoned his calling to marry, in secrecy, a widowed slightly older parishioner. Their affair began innocently enough with confessions and consultations transcending into infatuations and passions that became something quite intense. When discovered, the priest and his pregnant wife were immediately excommunicated and left their small town settling in the capital to have their child.

The child grew to be handsome and respectful. At a young age he fell in love with the less than pure yet exceptionally charming Alejandra Noemi Baez. During a hurricane he and his parents were forced to take shelter in Doña Pura Baez's home after nature's winds disassembled their house. The Baez house contained nearly one dozen modest bedrooms and the women who both resided and worked them, shared them unselfishly.

Fausto Manuel had known Alejandra all his life, but it was only when he saw her bathing outside in the fierce Caribbean rains that he became truly taken with her. The long yellow shirt she wore, a memento conceivably forgotten by some customer who had hastened home before his wife awoke and discovered the smell of his infidelity baking in the Sun's arrival. It adhered to her wet form as the skies poured onto her creamed skin. He could think of nothing else except her for months. Their parents arranged their first date and shortly after their wedding. The son of the ex-priest and impatient widow married to the exquisite daughter of the town Madam. When they had a child six months later, they named him Fausto Leandro.

They, the Batista's, were very much unlike the Lambargas who were from Barahona, a wealthier area in the southern regions of Quisqueya. He, Reynaldo Lambarga, was the son of a renowned military general who never was able to have a child with his stunning Castilian wife. She became inhibited over the years and crawled into herself. Perhaps from that loneliness, or lust, he began an affair with his Haitian servant, a young gifted bruja of Yoruban descent. She was tall, much taller than he with attractive almost Asiatic eyes and a pretty smile. Her broken Spanish was muddled and oftentimes confusing, but she aroused desires in him that his wife no longer chose to with her deep gyrating curves and smooth ebon skin that tasted better than anyone should. Such a relationship was taboo at the time of Trujillo,

el chivo,

especially when it involved a three-star general in the Haitian hating dictator's army. But not much after in that time, she was pregnant and bore his only child, a son named Reynaldo like his

father. The couple raised the humble child as their own but allowed the birthmother to serve as the nanny under the condition that she not tell him the truth, an agreement she swore to and broke when the child became seven. When he was told he immediately confronted his parents who admitted to the deception and then deported Ifita back to Haiti where she spent the rest of her days and grew to be exceptionally powerful in her craft. In a rocker, alone, she eventually died of a broken heart never bearing other children and never again seeing her son who would never again remember her.

Bellamaria Boutros, the sole heir to the Boutros sugar refineries had met Reynaldo son of Reynaldo the general at the age of thirteen. Though lightly intimidating, his fetching tall physical appearance attracted her and most of the young girls in school. She did her best to get his attention which she finally succeeded in doing some ten years later when as she would often put it,

> "he had eaten all the candies in the shop
> and hungered for something sweeter."

They were married and had their first and only child one year later naming her Yolandamari Lambarga. Five years later after a severe economic downfall following the Goat's assassination, they left everything for a fresh start in the United States taking with them their only remaining possession, their daughter.

Yoli and Leo met on the flight in from Areopuerto de Las Americas. It was their first plane-ride, and they were seated together so that their parents could smoke and talk in the back of the plane. Back then flying was a status achievement and done by a relative few. With the exception of Bellamaria none of them had ever been in the United States before and they decided to stay in touch so that at least they would know some other people in Nueva York besides their distant families.

It was a time when Quisqueyans were new to America.

Yoli was nervous, she held her doll close. It was made of beaten cotton with tribal stitching. Her name was Miosotis and she had been handed down for so long that nobody remembered her origin. Reynaldo suspected she was probably well over a couple hundred years old.

she tugged on the frills of
yoli's dress to whisper in her ear,

"he will love you more than a flower loves the rain and Sun, but he will become lost, he will not return to you in life."

As quickly as they were said Yoli forgot those words.

Leo introduced himself to the both of them, but Miosotis rolled her eyes and became inanimate. The children discussed how they had heard from second and third cousins who had visited New

York, that it was a place where everyone was rich and where single dollars were thrown away to make room for larger bills. She was only five years old, but even then Yolandamari Lambarga was infatuated, he however was deeply in love, and he told her that from moment she was his. Their parents arrived and eventually settled within minutes of each other. Over the years, they, the children, grew closer attending the same schools spending every day together. Leo was quite the little gentleman; he would have given his life to protect her because he loved her more than he did seeing and hearing and he did all things possible to show his affection as they grew together.

At twelve, Yoli developed into a beautiful shapely young girl. Boys and men alike would have drained their hearts to enter her circle, but she had only two passions, learning and Leo. Leo was tall and athletic, but never a great student unlike her, with much struggle he kept his grades at a passing average so that she would not get on his case so much and so that she would never grow ashamed of him. They held between them an innocent level of love that only heightened with everything they shared. Often, their parents would hint and even force them to associate with others,

widen their horizons.

But when they were separated, they both usually became very withdrawn almost ill. The parents changed tactics and decided to consolidate their efforts into making sure that they were aware that if they went too far at too young of an age, there would be a heavy price to pay.

On the day she turned fifteen Yoli was exactly five months pregnant, and Leo was working seventeen hours a day at the Ureña grocery on one-o-ninth and Columbus trying his best to be a man. They told her parents about her concealed pregnancy, *she was showing,*

she was given three months to move out. Leo was told the same, so he quit school to work seven full days a week in order to get an apartment and some cushion money. He worked so much that even though they were only a couple of blocks apart the two barely saw each other. Their parents understood the depth of their children's love, but it was agreed that they needed to accept responsibility for their actions. Leo was only partially able to put together a home for his family when Yoli went into labor. The birth was painless, but the ground trembled in the last moments before Fausto Leandro Jr. was introduced feet first into our world.

No one gave them gifts; nobody threw a shower for them. Their friends weren't allowed upstairs to visit them,

hospital age restrictions,

and were forced to disassociate with them by parents who feared infection. Their baby was born two months early and he only had eleven hundred dollars saved. Not enough for an apartment or most of the other things needed by an infant. Her belongings thrown in the street they moved into a tiny basement room in the Bronx.

There was little heat, and the water was not nearly drinkable due to the lead and coloring. They hung clothes when they could on exposed dry-rotted structural framing. Old women, long not remembered, looked languidly at them from the spaces in between. The bathroom and kitchen were outside the apartment and shared with two other rooms whose couples had similar realities and old women. They ate rice with eggs twice a day and were blessed in that Yoli breasts produced enough to feed the baby. He ventured all over from business to business searching for work, but his age got in the way even when he lied about it. The new family needed more money and Leo became convinced that the streets were the only option, Yoli disagreed, but could offer him no alternative. Leo linked up with a boy named Nefti who claimed a good way to make quick money was to simply stick-up those who had it. They began by robbing a number runner and then the sozzled and amorous customers at a gay bar on West 81st and Columbus. The money was decent, but it wasn't nearly enough, and Leo told him that he was looking for bigger things. A day later Nefti told him about a big job he'd lined up, he was supposed to come over, but he was gunned down and robbed in the lobby of his parents building as he checked the mail. The assailant was never caught, but it was generally believed to have been a contract killing paid for by the owner of the bar.

Leo searched for another source of income, so he got work as a lookout for a drug spot near Hunts Point, Chiqui Moet the spot's owner quickly took a liking to him and put him on a corner as a honeydrip. From six in the afternoon till about three in the morning Leo hustled. Yoli would bring him dinner and the baby around eight every night and they managed to move into an apartment with clean water and heat nearby. Things were looking up and Leo figured in three months or so he could leave the streets with enough money to stabilize in one home and maybe buy a union janitor or doorman's job from a superintendent in those fancy downtown Manhattan buildings.

He figured it would be safer and definitely more respectable, so that Yoli could be proud of him.

About one day and a month after Leo was supposed to leave the corner Yoli came by for her routine eight o'clock visit, she argued with Leo telling him that they had more than enough money and that it was time he quit. He argued but was quickly silenced by her temper. She left angry leaving behind only the piercing arctic silence that Latinas are capable of creating. Leo went into the corner bodega and spoke to Chiqui Moet telling him he would finish the week then leave.

Yoli walked to the playground as she usually did when she was upset and got on the swings with the baby in near view. She swung back and forth climbing higher and higher until she noticed a pockmarked berry-blue-eyed man standing to the left of her. Almost without hesitation she leaped off the swing grabbed the stroller and rushed home, she checked behind her, no one was there. A sigh of relief came, as she entered the building and then her apartment door. Yoli was home and safe and within an hour she and her son were bathed, in bed and asleep with her son only an exhale away.

The banging at the window came around midnight, Yoli was awakened by her baby's whimpers. She had always been a heavy sleeper in every sense with the sole exception of any movement or sound that her baby made. Juni, short for Junior, did not cry often, in fact he had only done it once since birth, so Yoli had conditioned herself to interpret every sound he made. This was the sound of fear and that terrified her; immediately she called the bodega and asked Chiqui Moet to get Leo. Chiqui put the phone down and headed towards the door but was sidetracked by one of his other workers who came in to re-up material and turn in cash. Yoli realizing that she was forgotten finally went to the toy chest and grabbed one of the toy guns her baby was too young to play with and walked slowly towards the window.

Hunched over in the darkness, trying repeatedly to ram a silver-necked screwdriver through the window lock was the large berry-blue-eyed man who had watched her in the playground. She, showing not the panic that was, that should have overwhelmed her, rushed up to the window and banged her fist against it with a force that shattered it, pointing the toy at the stranger who scrambled down the fire escape showered by shards. Yoli quickly grabbed her baby and locked herself in the bathroom. She held her baby as close to her as she could, the toy at her feet and a kitchen knife at rest against her leg. Leo arrived home about three hours later unaware of the night's events. Upon entering he saw the broken window and dashed to the room then through the house to find the locked bathroom door and them cuddled in silence. By morning he managed to coax her into telling him what had occurred. It took him six hours to find another apartment and furnish it.

Leaving everything behind he relocated them to their old neighborhood in upper Manhattan, a place he knew would help soothe his wife,

> *they weren't really married but being latin and living together is rarely perceived otherwise.*

They went to bed and at midnight he awoke and

left without waking her.

blue.

Leo returned to the Bronx and over to Chiqui
Moet's bodega and asked him why he didn't give
him the call. Chiqui Moet indifferently shrugged.
Chiqui Moet fell to the ground as the result of
the shot to the head. Leo then stormed out with
the material and money in hand. He went to
every junkie offering drugs for information on
the stranger. Finally, one old woman, a veteran
junkie nicknamed China, whose real name was
Gloria, agreed to take him directly to the
stranger. Right off of the Grand Concourse on
Rockwood was an old well-kept building, it was
there on the roof, kneeled before a small white
flame that he found the berry-blue-eyed man.

shirtless.

Even hunched over from the scarred back his
frame seemed massive, his braided hair was long
and nearly silver. Leo charged up behind him and
kicked him onto the bum fire.

The stranger fell but stood almost as quickly, dropping a screwdriver. His size towered over Leo who could see his own reflection in the strangers' luminescing eyes. Breathing heavily, he giggled, he ran. Leo picked up the screwdriver and chased him down the stairs stabbing at his back every few steps. In one stroke it became lodged within his spine.

The stranger ran and Leo ran after him stopping only to rip a fire emergency axe from its' encasing on the staircase forgetting the about the gun he'd already used. He swung the axe just as they reached the street ripping into the stranger's back, dislodging the screwdriver and again knocking him down. He dragged himself, but Leo struck him down on his side flipping him over. He hacked into the stranger's chest, repeatedly even as the thick blood splashed drenching Leo's face and body. Leo wouldn't, couldn't ... stop. The dark thick blood had splattered into his mouth and the warm salted sweetness only enraged him more. Mercilessly he swung onto the body, he swung onto the body...

he swung onto the body...

before finally, he stopped and walked home dropping the axe, arriving just before the Sun's morning rupture, the blood dried in clumps on his skin and clothes. He told Yoli what had occurred as she removed his clothing and washed his skin with water, soap and the tears that flung themselves from her lengthy eyelashes. His clothes were taken to the boiler room and burned, and the two lay in bed quietly watching television with Juni asleep between them. The news came on and the coverage of the incident reported the drug overdose of an old woman whose body was found lying in a huge pool of serpent's blood, a word *Azules* was carved onto the woman's chest. There was also a murder of a suspected honeydrip in Hunts Point who was found with similar writing on his forehead, an inch or so above where the screwdriver was jammed. Leo sprung out of bed and ran into the bathroom, he gazed at the mirror. He was trembling and he could again taste the salted sweet. Heading to the kitchen pulled out the drugs that he had buried in the rice container and returned to the bathroom where he spiked a massive hit. The heroin then cocaine painfully streaked into his bloodstream and ripped over his vertebrae into his brain. Changed, he giggled as he looked up at his watch, it was seconds after midnight as he sang to himself.

"happy birthday...
happy birthday"
   he was sixteen.

                                        ...BERRY BLUE

CHAPTER 25

"what would you have me tell him?"

"anything... nothing... it will not
matter."

"what if he says no?"

"he may... he may not... it will not
matter."

"how will I find him?"

"walk and you will find him. he
stands on a star feeding the
hungry."

Giovanni Miotan looked like the grandchild of his
contemporaries. He was strong, unweathered,
and elegant. When his wife's senility finally
collapsed into dementia, and she was placed into
full time compassionate care some twenty years
prior, there she died, his hand in hers.

he hoped that she knew.

His friends and relatives accused him of having
made covenants with the devil.

> *a man who has outlived his*
> *children should not remain*
> *beautiful with age.*

They said so even as the loneliness infected him
with insomnia. It was not long after the flesh was
long gone from her bones, and the signs of wear
became evident on her stone, that he at last
stopped setting her place and serving her meals.
Nightly, he would eat silently, then pack up her
serving and venture out to whatever house of
worship. Once there he would give her plate to
whichever hungry woman he found there.

It was there that she found him.

Giovanni handed her the plate and she ate it
with her fingers and then dropped the plate.
Each slopping chew was wet and grinding. She
wiped her face with the heel of her palm and
stood. The woman extended her arm and took

his. Her thumb and index around his wrist and
her remaining fingers pressed to his lifeline,

    his lifeline,

she led him away from his place settings and his
past.

Giovanni searched for words. The years
consisted of mostly listening. He was only
allowed to speak on Sabbath days and only after
his second soul settled in.

> "for a day El numbs man's second soul on
> the eve of every one hundred and forty
> forth hour so that you might be enabled
> to comprehend what you are conditioned
> not to see?"

It is forgotten that for six of the last seven days
of gestation all infants develop twin souls,

    more fraternal than identical.

The absence of both causes a stillbirth, of one...
madness.

        ...RESTED SOULS

CHAPTER 26

the misconception about ghosts is
that they exist to haunt or
fulfill some unknown greater
purpose.
alternate facts at best.
ghosts exist,
in the realm of they who are
dead, the instantaneous meeting
of eyelids amounts to about a
chiliad. if a living dies, even
if only moments before decided,
the point of crossover changes
relative time and movement. a
moment becomes more. haunting
and all the other mischief of the
undead are just a way of
distracting themselves. there is
actually no such thing as time
only movement so if there is no

DON'T SEE WE

motion the man-made concept of time
will seemingly be still.

Startled by the screaming, Fausto fell from his bed and ran towards the bathroom. He kicked in the door just in time to see Annie shatter the vapor-clad medicine cabinet mirror with her fists. She stood unclothed, shivering, her hair white, and her hands dripping blood and water. Fausto wrapped her thin frame in a white bath towel and carried her over to the bedroom where he cleaned and wrapped her bleeding hands and feet. Shaking, at times uncontrollably, Annie told him of how as she painted the rest of her body, Leo reached through the mirror, embracing her. His mouth pressed to her ear, she could feel the dissipating heat off his words,

warm,

"tell him he is of age, i can't hide
him any longer. despite what he sees
evil stands behind him."

The apparition shoved her away as it was pulled

back by its' skin into steamed glass, only her fogged reflection remained. Fausto didn't react but he listened, assuming nothing. When she at last slept, Fausto watched her hair return to its' original flaxen strawberry color and her fair-skin absorbed the blue paint, the scabbing already forming on her hands.

Time appeared to pass and La Bodeguita's extended into parts of Connecticut and Massachusetts. There was some distribution to Ohio, but only by third party. Shipments for La Bodeguita from Mexico usually came in as far as North Carolina and they were by land.

The Pinzon Cartel was more experienced and adept at smuggling. They used low flying planes, pirated yachts, and bellies full of cocaine filled condoms to bring it over. Over the years both used a number of unique but short-lived tricks like sausages, soda cans, dogs and babies. The bolder Tian Di Hui, brought in mass quantities of dope using indebted countrymen and legitimate shipping operations. Their logic was that the countless huge shipments easily overwhelm any anti-drug efforts. All used the New York Waterway at varying times,

when the mob accepted bids and awarded use of the docks.

It took time, but eventually the Bratva made their contribution to the game and helped transcend drug smuggling. Old retrofitted Soviet subs were purchased and driven by a cooperative of former naval commanders.

La Bodeguita leased local routes from leftover Sicilians who guaranteed safe travel along them. The Fis were chipping away at their grip, but that was their issue and it never interfered with the business. They taxed reasonably for the tolls, soon they were making enough money from the routes that betrayal was unprofitable. The Pakhans and Brigadiers would not work with them directly anyway. Everybody got paid dutifully including those in governments. Haiti alone was seeing over eighty million US$ a year just for use of their runways, another ten million went in operational costs.

> *it seems like a lot, but just a few days ago some clown made a bad drop and 467 bricks were lost, that almost seven million US$ wholesale. it was written off.*

These things were secrets from the many unaware of their illusions. To believe that anything substantial consistently invaded this country or those it controls without approval from at least one of the powers that run it is childlike. All would stop within days of a decision to do so, but it won't, it would choke economies if it did, Miotan had taught him that.

Few things were worthy challengers to the color and power of money,

> *no matter how many lights are on the world's eyes only focus when a candle is intentionally lit in front of a camera.*

CHAPTER 27

The sandwich thumped on the counter.

"how the hell can you eat that?"

"blimpies is awesome
beal, you got nooooo
idea."

"putting that much crap on a sandwich
can't possibly be good for you. It can't be
good for anyone."

"whatever… whatever…
you won't try it so you
won't get it."

Fausto shoulders the glass door open followed
by Beal.

"now what?"

"i just gotta go collect
real quick."

"why are you doing that shit? you should
have someone doing that!"

"beal relax I'm
kidding. blimpies
doesn't sell good-o."

"not funny fausto, there's enough going
on without you aggravating me."

Fausto chuckled and continued towards the
store. In front of it a swarthy bald man wearing
curiously snug purple pants and a baby blue
wife-beater laid on his belly with a huge piece of
colored chalk.

more orange.

He painstakingly rubbed shades into the
concrete creating a Mediterranean midday sun.
As they exited, Beal tossed a fifty into the
artist's bucket.

"really?"

"a society without art ceases to be a society fausto."

Suddenly, in an effort to slip the soda into his pocket while simultaneously gripping the sandwich, the latter lost stability and fell to the ground. Fausto stared at it, heartbroken as the ratbirds landed seemingly from nowhere and quickly jabbed in their disease-dusted beaks.
A strange short Eurasian looking man named Giovanni Miotan approached Fausto. His presence commanded disturbed respect, Fausto followed his instincts and agreed to meet with him. Mr. Miotan spoke of monies and economies and explained to them how that the dark markets were as essential to driving the world economy as technology was. That those who truly controlled the world were the descendants of the Nephalem,

those unspoken.

The unknown variable that so many blamed for the world's ills and turmoil.

"that's a whole lotta
bullshit you're
throwing at me man."

"fausto! mas respeto please."

"oh come on beal.
this cat is selling
us a bunch of
conspiracy bullshit.
what's next black
helicopters and
computer chips
implanted at birth?"

"young one i understand your skepticism. but
the world is more connected than you think and
will only become more so."

"mr. miotan, why not
pick someone older if
this is all true."

"i did not choose."

"i apologize for fausto's
outburst sir."

"he is young still mr. beal."

...*BLIMPIES AND BULLSHIT*

CHAPTER 28

Cocaine,

    perico,

was, is, a sloppier market than the almighty H, H, h,

    dope, manteca, heroin,

and it generates less long term. Users of the nose candy tend to burn out.

> "newcomers have more trouble breaking into h. the startup costs are higher and customers are loyal. look at how long it takes us to put together spots. think about it son, cali, medellin, the mendozas in oaxaca, they're all pumping millions into opium crops… bringing in talent from the golden triangle… the middle east."

> > "yeah beal but they are producing shit. how many cases of that

fucking lemon extract
are we using to cut that
tar you got us into a
couple of months ago."

"i understand but trust me on this, they
will get better at it. these baseheads only
last a couple of years and coke users fall
apart after like five six. mantequeros are
long term."

They went back and forth for weeks, but Beal
got his way. La Bodeguita gradually began
revamping so that it could gear towards just
heroin. They already had a couple of decent
stamps, SpiceKandi was the more popular, it was
no DayNight, but it held its own. Many insisted
that cocaine not be cast aside. Perico was still
huge.
Designer drugs like MDMA, Special K, several
uses of embalming fluid, Meth, and others were
of little interest to Fausto and his partners.

Overall small-time hustlers were too small to be
taken seriously. They were bottom feeders.

Then
came
Lantigua.

Lantigua was different,
deep pockets,
well supplied,
for the moment unknown.
He heisted shipments and wiped out a dozen
Bodegueros. Something changed. Death and lost
shipments happen, and they have to be factored
into the books as projected losses, they are
accepted industry risks, shrinkage. Still this
surge was far removed. Truth be told only
twenty-three groups actually control the world
drug trade,
         thirteen in the americas,
and it takes at least half a decade to build a

hyper-extended organization. Rises don't go unnoticed. Power, all power exchanges hands as a result of simple opportunity. In this thing they can come under the guise of prosecutions, murder, and war.

La Bodeguita generated well, and such success was appreciated.

A meeting was arranged.

Morning came and Fausto became violently ill, vomiting blood and collapsing. Some men along with Annie took him to the Doctors Hospital across from Gracie Mansion and Beal continued on as planned believing the meeting was crucial. Fausto could catch up in a day or so. All else went as planned as Beal sat next to Miotan and began discussing possible ways of stopping the problems as the flight ascended into the sky. They were white-noised by a group of youngsters carousing and singing in French. Annie tried to rush the lab as the medical staff gawked at her blue skin, which she did not explain. Fausto had just fallen asleep when the doctor came in to wake him with the results. He asked that all leave the room, and all did with the exception of Annie who insisted on staying.

CHAPTER 29

symbols that looked like numbers, but were not, were drawn on his back, neck, and palms using blue oil. dressed only in torn rags he was given a fistful of small moist bitter blue leaves to chew, as he stood centered in a lightless oblong room. he remained motionless as instructed.

fucking cats everywhere. gradually it grew warmer, sweat began to dampen the silk scarf on his head and finally a drop fell and hissed as it hit the floor. from it a scorching heat spread engulfing everything and blasting until the room was converted into screaming white tongues. a blazing tunnel formed and led beyond view, it burned more as he panicked and tried to run, so weakly,

he walked. in his head all he could think
of was songs from his childhood.
the flames whipped at and slashed his
feet, even his hair burned. the dye on
his skin crackled. fausto could see the
end and upon reaching it, it smothered
him, and he blacked out from the pain.
he awoke to find himself crouched on
a blank marble tombstone in a
graveyard at dawn, the soil around
him disturbed. his body coated in
ashes, his skin still burning.

When his fever broke and he awoke drenched,
the Doctor was standing at his bedside.

"young man you are a healthy nineteen
year old. all your test are negative but one,
why was reptile blood in your stomach?
preliminary tests identify it as snake blood
and of not just one, but various types all

mixed together."

Fausto was dumbfounded and unable to respond from the shock. He could only manage to shrug in confusion.

> "we are going to keep you overnight for observation, but my guess is that you are fine and can go in a couple of days."

He then left the room as Annie kissed Fausto's forehead and ran out to thank the doctor. Fausto laid in the quiet room finally willing the strength to reposition the bed and turn on the television. The sports wrap-up was just beginning, The Red Sox won and were going to the World Series then an interruption by a special report on a crashed UXB flight. He bit his lower lip and watched as they announced the horrific crash of Flight 1600, spit spilled over his bottom lip in a long string as he silently

screamed, straining as he heard the news.
Dozens of witnesses interviewed off the Long
Island Sound described a glowing projectile
streaking towards the plane moments before
the explosion. Fausto flicked off the television,
Beal was dead.

...TIPPY TOES

CHAPTER 30

Bloodshed is a method.

Bloodshed is a method and always effective fertilizer for the raising of fear. Miami, Boston, and Philadelphia were completely overrun, Bodegueros were caught off guard and the Cubans lost twenty years' worth of hierarchy. The initial assaults were so huge, random, and violent that it was impossible to fend them off or predict their patterns. Workers were ill prepared for the mercenaries that were coming at them. Lantigua punctured the south and was beginning to make moves in New York. Seven months and La Bodeguita was again running on skeleton crews. But no one had seen Fausto. Lantigua was receiving shipments weekly and the number of overdoses was entering into the dozens with the purity of the dope he was putting out. To strengthen addictions, he used greater purity then cut it slowly over time so that people would

buy more to get the same effect. It was an old practice of hustling, and it was working in Philadelphia, and it would work in New York. Authorities panicked, and in an effort to regain some public confidence, arrested or shot anyone that looked remotely suspicious. Chaos was everywhere and everyone was armed and afraid as much of life as of death. Public outcry was common, community leaders were missing with feeling the powerlessness that third or lesser world nations had grown numb to.

Bad times exacerbate abuse and times were bad. Now out of the shadows Lantigua strongarmed his way into several profitable areas in major cities. An admitted Lolitaphile, he had a strong and distinct taste for the young girls of the 11 to 15 age range. Often taking whichever terrorized child he liked. On one occasion, a horde led by an enraged father named Rafael Aguadulce attempted to kill him after his eleven-year-old daughter Lila was taken and raped.

Lantigua's men quickly slaughtered the group, he tortured the father for three days using pliers and wire cutters to mangle his gums, ears, and genitalia before he mercifully slit the man's throat. His mutilated body was hung from a light pole on one-sixth-eight street and Broadway as a warning. He comically spun upside down slowly by a single leg.

Smuggled in from Holland, Australia, and Israel the club drug MDMA was being forcefully given to any pretty girl Lantigua's men could find over the age of ten. They believed it seasoned them sexually, making their enslavement more bearable. Many of the older ones were put out on the streets as prostitutes, a side business that Lantigua allowed his closest men to run for extra cash, others were kept for personal use, some were never seen again. Feared, an amoral madman was roaming free to shatter the lives of whomever he pleased. The police were weakened by cowardly and corrupt politicians.

The Nephalem wanted havoc, it allowed them to manipulate various economies further weakening their opposition and multiplying their profit. Lantigua gave them the disruptive force needed to cause a lack of confidence in all those institutions that Americans held dear. Suffering was flooding homes until nothing was left of respect and hope.

...A FEW NEPHALEM AND THE LOLITAPHILE

CHAPTER 31

On the evening of the day her father was cut down and buried in a closed casket Lila and her best friend kneeled before an open bible while they faced each other, both dressed alike, both of them victims of Lantigua. They hugged and began to press sleeping pills out from their foil packs and into a white ceramic bowl they had mailed away for after saving proofs of purchase from their favorite cereal. Four boxes in total, ninety-six pills. When finished one of them got up, picked up and threw away the empty cartons and foils while the other went to the kitchen only to be met a moment later by her friend. They returned with a large glass of milk and a bottle of Bosco, patiently and carefully sitting down as they had done before. Together they squeezed the thick syrup into the bowl and onto the pills. Slowly they fed one another the pills, placing them one at a time in each other's mouths swallowing them easily with the milk until they became so drowsy that they could not continue. The two then hugged and fell asleep slipping out of consciousness,

out of life.

They were discovered later by Lila's mother who had been up to that moment sedated and in bed. The next day at the local church in an open casket the two were placed in the same coffin in the same sleeping embrace they had died in. It was thought that they could keep each other company as they had in life. The children, in their identical pretty, white cotton, ruffled dresses, were surrounded by their stuffed animals, toys and dolls. The toys shared the saddened expressions present among the mourners as they came up and paid their respects. One by one, they hesitantly came up to the coffin, some weeping others shocked and straining to breathe. When the casket was finally

closed, taken to, and placed into the grave that
would keep their bodies forever,

      or land value determined otherwise,

two identical stars appeared in the daylight sky
and then faded as the night approached.

CHAPTER 32

Immediately after leaving the hospital Fausto and Annie boarded a private flight in New Jersey bound for Quisqueya. Upon landing they were met by Edmonds, a tall muscular dark-skinned man who drove them to a beachfront resort. It was named La Shoshanna Naedez after its' owner, and it was one of those places where people with power and money went to drop from public view. Fame no longer existed once one entered the vast property; one was just another king or queen in search of plush treatment.

The owner was an old woman who in her youth had been the paramour to the dictator otherwise known as the Butcher of the Caribbean. The dictator had met her when she came to him to beg for her incarcerated brother's life. He granted her the request but wanted her virginity in exchange, she agreed, and he wasted no time in taking it. Throughout the world many people have many abilities, but Shoshanna's gift was her sexuality, once it was awakened she crippled him with her passion, using him as he had used her, never bearing him a child.

He remained obsessed with her until his alleged death and as a result he made her very wealthy. She took all the money he'd given her over the years and opened Casa Shoshanna Naedez as a resort in hopes of attracting the wealthy elite she had encountered during her affair, but after Trujillo's removal she was excommunicated by them and viewed as a glorified whore. Fortunately for the outcast she attracted other outcasts from all parts of the world, somehow the wealthy black sheep became aware of the resort. In response she perfected the art of catering to their needs, creating a paradise where the law and judgment were non-issues. Hence presidents and gangsters ate, associated, and negotiated freely.

Cameras were banned.

Her policy was whatever you wanted you could have as long as it didn't violate anyone else. No violence. No kids. She never billed anyone for anything, one was to pay what he or she felt was adequate. This resulted in her resort receiving outrageously huge sums of money for their multitude of services that were to say the least unique. La Shoshanna fulfilled a need. That is why perhaps prophetically, Beal made sure that Fausto was aware of its existence and purpose.

Annie was led to a room where she found a modest wardrobe of clothing and a set of car keys. She speedily changed into a skimpy bikini and rushed down to the beach for a swim and sunbath. Passersby gathered and stared at the tanning blue skinned beauty. Edmonds walked to the beach with Fausto and sat at a table a few yards from the water. They ordered some roasted shrimp and drinks, Fausto quickly glanced over at Annie.

"you know faust she has been blue for so long that i honestly can't remember what she was like before."

"she is still your typical long island girl."

"kid, she may be a lot of things, but typical is not one of them. anyway i hear all hell is breaking loose over there, that's good. i'm glad you're here, you needed to go already while you're still alive and young. you should move here."

"nah ricki, not this way, these are animals. they don't respect nuthin or no one,

if i let them...

i can't let them.

i actually need you

to help me."

edmonds squished together his

curiously thick eyebrows and growled

out,

"help you do fucking what? answer me...

what!?

i am no filthy dealer faust,

i am, i was a soldier

and i've done enough shit to preserve

your shit.

you are lucky i did what i did."

fausto took a long sip from

his rum and ice,

"ricki,

you taught me a long
time ago that
there are degrees of
evil. you once told me
the right evil could be
used to create a
good. i know you and
you know me,
i came to you because
i have no one else,
there is no one else.
beal would agree with
me."

"beal! beal! you little motherfucker! he
only stuck around because he was trying
to save you and look at what happened
to him!
he's dead and don't kid yourself you
selfish fuck,
you killed him."

flinging the glass into the closest
palm, fausto moved up to edmonds,

"fuck you! fuck you!
fuck you!
i loved that man
like a father, and you
fucking know it! you don't
need to tell me,
i know what happened.
i got no choice! help
me or don't,
i'll figure it out,
don't fucking lecture me
about right and wrong
because right now your
words don't mean jackshit
to me!
i carry enough shit!"

"you know who else loved him like a

father?

his kids,

and now he's gone.

that's on you. live with it.

how you do that is going to make you."

Ricardo stood and walked away. Fausto waited.
He glanced over to Annie who had flipped over
and fallen asleep as the child who normally only
collected bottles earned an easy $50 by
coating her with SPF 70.

"oye! chamaquito!

cuidado con tus

manos!"

"i speak english,

he responded to fausto.

she pay me to rub her, ok!"

"whatever little

man just watch

those hands."

twenty minutes later,

"have them here in three days, and I don't
want no bullshit."

...SHE PAY ME TO RUB HER, OK

CHAPTER 33

Nearly one hundred men arrived on buses at the
makeshift training base in the cold mountainside
of Constanza. The area was beautiful, and the
air was cool and thin.

Light snowflakes fell sparingly, never quite
landing, almost as though they knew they were
out of place. The grass grew green all around in
defiance of the cold. As the four buses came to
a complete stop Edmonds ran into each of them
screaming.

> "get off the fucking bus now! get off this
> heap of shit and line up facing me."

Most rushed into a sloppy formation, Juanbestia
spit on the ground when Edmonds spoke.
Edmonds walked up to him and told him to cut
the shit. Juanbestia, a manager and occasional
enforcer, ignored Fausto's callings for him to
shut-up and lunged.

Taking a swing with his right arm, he was blocked, grabbed, and pulled inward. Edmonds stepped left then right and slammed him to the ground using that foot for leverage and the left to kick him in the kidneys causing immobilization, inhaling first he thrusted a last blow over Juanbestia's heart causing it to skip.

> "let me make this clear, you came here by choice… that was the end of your say in the matter. you will not leave until you either complete this or die, and to prove that this is not a joke fausto will be joining you."

From his chair Fausto looked over at him, goofy and perplexed. Edmonds went to him.

> *in a low voice*,

> "line up you little shit or i walk."

He looked at him, humbled conceding that the soldier had gotten the better of him, he marched as well as he could and got into formation. No one questioned Ricardo Edmonds after that.

The training was itself referred to as Shock Training and it consisted of, among other things, an intense series of stamina building activities. Before breakfast they ran three miles, Fausto had difficulty keeping up, so he was chosen as the Road Guard. This meant he would run up ahead of the others and stop traffic while they all passed then he would run up ahead again to repeat the activity. The purpose of this military position was to build up the stamina and strength of the weakest link therefore eliminating it. It also served in the prevention of accidents during early-morning and late-night runs. The others had always been a lot more active than the boss so they had an advantage. All were given black sweatpants and t-shirts and were taught to march. Hundreds of push-ups by the end of the first week and the workouts were getting more and more intense including fireman carries and various other grass drills. One exercise consisted of eight men carrying a heavy log and running for half a mile then slowing down to walk while they switched sides and then running back. They went to bed about midnight and awoke at 5am. Hand to hand combat training was vicious and often resulted in at least one injury and a few shattered egos. Fausto excelled. They took classes learning maps of roads, sewers, small weapons, and knives. Most agreed that the hardest part of it all was the gas tent, a huge airtight tent filled with CN gas, which they were required to enter in teams of three. A small metal dish filled with the powdered CN was placed on top of a burning candle. As it burned it saturated the air inside and the men entered with gas masks, which they had to remove. Coughing would begin followed by burning eyes and noses, wheezing, vomiting, gagging, and choking. It felt as though one's body fluids were siphoning out through the nose and mouth. Many described it as drowning in clouds of burning air. It became vogue among them to take polaroids of one another covered in mucus.

Time progressed, they advanced into warfare training and weapons. No man was ever left behind during any exercise and all of them pushed.

Mornings later, a rooster bayed its' ingratitude at the Sun, but as usual everyone was already awake. Edmonds stood before them.

> "you
>
> will
>
> kill.
>
> you will kill them because they've lived too fucking long and done too much. and let's not bullshit, so have we. you get shot. you're bleeding out. you take one of them with you. you're cornered with an empty gun? you bash

heads.

they don't go home, they don't go to jail.

let whatever what was willing to love

them scream when they've seen what

done to them.

these last days are for you enjoy. don't

attract too much attention. i'll see you

back in a few days."

They ran to the awaiting cabs and motoconchos.
Fausto walked towards Edmonds.

"thanks ricki,

you know for

what you did here."

"i hope i did the right thing, you know

they are ready for pretty much anything

fausto."

The groups partied hard in San Francisco de

Macoris, Boca Chica, Cuidad Quisqueya, Bonao,

and San Pedro. All arrived a day early knowing
the severity of what lay ahead. They lay on the
beach allowing the warm night breezes to fondle
them. Leaping into the resting ocean at any
given time, drunk on coquettish women,

> *and men in couple of cases,*

 the wonder that surrounded them, and the
cerveza they consumed in huge near sickening
quantities,

> *the countless empty bottles fed the*
> *local poor for days. they did little for*
> *the dozen or so eggs left inseminated.*

...MOTOCONCHOS AND 5 LOBES FULL OF CN GAS

CHAPTER 34

Ricardo was a highly disciplined fetching type of dude, dark with endlessly deep eyes. A veteran of numerous special operations who'd trained Afghanis for anti-Soviet combat during the cold war, hunted undesirables in the Philippines and Lebanon, and neutralized difficulties in Nicaragua. Without much fan-fare he was forced out of the military, his commanding officers' homosexuality never exposed.

Ricki would have gone on to accomplish greater things had he not been discovered. A year later such an action on the part of the military was made illegal. He was Beals' closest friend and a reluctant uncle of sorts to Fausto.

Beal brought him to the States as a boy, while on a visit home a young boy named Ricki asked to shine his shoes. Beal declined but was confronted with a compelling argument. He was so impressed that he paid off some people and brought the boy and his family over to the U.S. and helped them build a new life.

...DON'T ASK DON'T TELL

CHAPTER 35

Seated next to each other, again watching Annie cause yet another spectacle on the beach.

"it is time you met beal's family."

Tremendous sigh,

> "think he was
> ashamed?
> of me i mean,
> is that why he never
> spoke of his family?
> why i never met anybody."

"kid, i do not know, when you die ask him."

The drive was bumpy, and Fausto was careful not to spill his cup. Some loud-ass merengue was blasting on the radio as they whooshed and whooshed by palm trees.

nervous.

This was the family that he so often wondered about; the secret Beal never shared.

> "there are two, chito is ten and a pain in the ass and then t h e r e ' s angie, my god-daughter."

> "how old is she?"

> "dunno. fifteen maybe, she is sweet, like her father, but tough and pretty like her mother...
> the house is right around... ahh here."

It wasn't a large home. It embodied Beal. As they walked up the driveway, he wondered to himself what would they think of him, would they blame him for Beal's death?

like ricardo did.

Edmonds knocked on the door and a boy yanked it open; he smiled as looked up and went running and yelling.

"llegaron! llegaron!"

A beautiful woman,

> *just continuously beautiful,*

came out and hugged Ricki, then looked at
Fausto. The amber apertures of her souls made
him want to apologize. She placed her hand to
his face. Her perfect arms wrapped around him,
and she sobbed softly as they embraced with
the longing that a mother would have for a son
believed himself forgotten. Not a said word,
somehow this was right.

"you are exactly as nori described you.
hermoso, con el aire de un principe,
i remember
when he say that to me.
my name is nati,
come meet the children,

this is chito who you already meet

and angie,

chito

busca tu hermana pa que conozca al famoso

fausto!"

The room imploded to silence when she entered
behind her brother. Moving without intention.
She was lovely, so innately raw she would have
driven sons of El to renounce their birthright for
her. She smiled and took Fausto's hand,

> *she was fucking fearless,*
> *the edges of her fingers were so soft.*

Her voice resonating from deep within her
diaphragm,

> "hello my name
> is angela
> and am pleased to
> finally meet you

after knowing you like all
my life."

Her eyes away for a moment,

blossom honey like her mother's,

they burned into Fausto, everything then failed
to interrupt. Her hands moved gracefully with
every word she spoke.
Touching

nati whispered to ricki,

"nori alway say when
they meet they going fall in love,
that is why he keep them apart,
so they no fall in love too soon."

While the others talked in the house they sat on
old mahogany rocking chairs outside, speaking
only in bits and pieces but saying more. A sliver
of Moon peaked at them with anticipation, as did
Chito. They went for a walk, thirty paces later
his upper lip to her lower, they felt themselves

belonging to one sempiternal beat. When they slipped from the bliss they again breathed.

"fausto we gotta go."

Fausto looked back towards Ricki,

"i have to go but i'll be back."

Angie placed her hand on his face and gently directed it back to hers.

"say it."

"i'll be back soon i promise."

"fausto!"

His head snapped back in the direction of the house.

"he's getting impatient,
i gotta..."

Again, she took his face and redirected it towards her,

"i can't see

your words

if you don't look at me."

He realized.

She continued,

"we have traded

secrets you and i."

Fausto took her hand and extended her fingers.

Pulling a ballpoint from his pocket he delicately

wrote on her forearm,

yesterday i knew nothing of you, today,

nothing exists without you.

He then walked her back and wished he'd kissed

her before he climbed into the awaiting vehicle.

...MY SOUL NOTICED WHAT I NEEDED.

CHAPTER 36

"When men became plentiful on the earth, and daughters were born to them, the sons of El, looking at the daughters of men, saw they were pleasing, so, they married as many as they chose. El said,

> *'My spirit must not forever be disgraced in man,*
> *for he is flesh;*
> *his life shall last no more than a hundred and twenty years.'*

The Nephilim were then onto the earth when the sons of El resorted to the daughters of man,
and had children by them."
Bible

Its' parts had been placed so that the Sun and later Moon could reflect,

with equal regularity,

on every surface inside as they faced the

observer. The outside would appear to glow through the unpolished sandglass brick exterior. A basilica made entirely of clear, opaque, and looking glass. L'église du Verre et des Miroirs was closed for immediate emergency repairs and the archdiocese extended a special thanks to the anonymous benefactor who would fund the work. It was important that the public not know that a killing had caused the Archbishop to be relocated outside Quebec. After a few millennia of inbreeding, the targets had evolved into a rather small number of humanesque-like beings with an absurd strength and intelligence. An abominable elite, who'd earned their ranks through tests of analytical and mathematical capability. The final test being the challenge and defeat of their parents in hand-to-hand combat. He was to hunt them, then in prescribed ritualistic manner burn their eyes, ears, tongues,

he used a culinary torch,
a modern take on a searing poker,

then he collected their thumbs and index
fingers. They were faced down spread eagle
facing north so that their souls could not rise.
They were the descendants of the pre-biblical
Nephilim; the inbreeding had helped them
maintain limited traits. They evolved into
immense slow moving puissant folks who thrived
on control and were strengthened by the
angelically plagued blood.

The leadership deeply entrenched itself and
based their operations deep in the Montreal
Basilica's lower levels right under the exhalations
of the Archbishop. Staff members were
implanted and served as their security and
informants.

By the week's end he'd penetrated the Le Tour
du Dieu. He moved through the minster and was
able to hide in Le Chambre du Reflexion. During
the day he read from the archives to pass the
time. Much seemed improbable. There was a chill
from emanating relics. One book, massive in

size, sealed and bound in glass panes with Aramaic text written in what appeared to be blood on sheets of Asian silk, it bared no title. The summary attached to it said it was discovered in a Taino Zemi shrine by a nameless conquistador somewhere in the fifteen hundreds. After a perfunctory analysis by experts,

experts,

the temple was subsequently razed. The book survived the flames. It remained warm to the touch, translations followed but formed frost when he read it out loud. It listed the formulas that were screamed out by the Elders to imprison the Suns long before the great compression. An indigenous woman appeared from within, absent of light, and placed three fingers on his lips, shaking her head as she slowly closed the tome.

Edmonds replaced it. He eventually found composure but was only further lost as to the righteousness of his task which he felt obligated to complete.

> *edmonds*
>
> *chose*
>
> *never to speak of it.*

Unable to leave the safe area, all were at peak strength when killed. Edmonds slaughtered them as they traveled in pairs and then one. Nothing had prepared them for an attack by a simple being, they knew only of enemies with gifts like theirs. Humans were spiritually stagnant talking apes to them. He tore down their mercenary guards like Yemaya's waters would a sandcastle. A loud snap echoed through the gothic halls with walls as the face peered at him and then closed its' eyes, it cracked again as he placed the head. Taking his time, he followed the instructions, the thirteen butchered were mutilated and positioned as ordered. On the eleventh night Edmonds left Quebec.

The furtive residences and carnage were

discovered days later due to the stench and word reached the Archbishop who without Vatican authorization ordered an investigation by a strand of Jesuits. When informed of their identities he ordered their bodies incinerated and a full investigation of the staff. He demanded that they take all steps necessary to rid themselves of the concern. Soon after, a series of staffing changes occurred underneath the crystal ceilings of the basilica.

A month after his return, Edmonds was visited at his home by a group of monks who informed him that he would be permitted to live only if he partook in a ceremonial oath of silent allegiance to the church. It was not a secret that he was allowed this luxury only because of the Craft. The ritual was recited in Illyrian,

> *the language of alexander of macedonia,*

in order to maintain a level of confusion in anyone who should eavesdrop on the rarely performed incantations, which dated before Christianity. Over his heart a marking was carved onto his chest symbolizing San Miguel, the entity they believed responsible for the deaths. It was believed that he was merely a vessel used by the archangel to eliminate the threat to El's Church.

That night Ricki went to bed knowing that the next day he would call and unchain Fausto on his enemies. A master of carnage himself, he recognized in Fausto a capability for viciousness greater than most.

...PURGE

CHAPTER 37

There is an adjoined stillness in death, it makes
the soul frantic. The waiting area became
inundated with they who are dead in the last
few years. Fewer people perceived their favors
anymore. The boy had long since been saved,
and as with the living, they who are dead now
crowded the space outside the kitchen.

> *crowding really sucks for they who are*
> *dead. their use of space is multi-*
> *existent in that a single spot,*
> *irrelevant of size, can hold an infinite*
> *number of residents.*

The doorbell screeched. A tween girl wearing
doorknocker earrings walked towards the door
from somewhere deep in the apartment. She
opened and let Fausto in, offering him a seat
with her hand.

Discretely, she walked away. The spirits hid
dozens to a crevice,

their sight turning into a kaleidoscope
of images with each added,
terrified of what he might or might not be. His
name was once whispered on the river and it
was rumored that he could introduce pain in
death, even without a hell. But he could not see
them and when he was called into the room, he
sat quietly as Margaro Osmin stared into the
water.

"at our most basic, we are the
supernatural units of an eventful life. this
is an opportunity... opportunities you will
have to change the path you walk. the
heartbeat you have recently discovered is
the first in a step in the tangled journey
on which you are destined to embark.
prepare, prepare mijo because it will..."
his sigh was emotional and lengthy
assume nothing."
Clueless, Fausto made his way to the

vehicles downstairs.

nothing,

until he hears from ricardo.

The men trained under Edmonds who'd taught them well. Still, there was the tension.
Some were anxious, others vengeful but all were scared of what was likely only hours away.
Fausto spent his time thinking of Angie. Time dragged on its' belly; it seemed like weeks since they met yet he could not bring himself to write her. Some days later, Annie, unaware of the details of the situation, sensed Fausto's frustration.

"faufi what is wrong
with you?
you haven't been
the same since you got back?"

"no"

Knowing her boundaries she went and ran him a hot bath. It was something she'd always done, if he chose, he could discuss it later with her,

never did.

As he sat in the steaming water scattered ideas
drifted through his mind. Thoughts of Angie
dominated.

was always going to love her.

Mist began to collect around the full- length
looking glass behind the door. Out of it formed
Leo, then Yoli.
She was as she was in photos, before Fausto
could remember her. He remained frozen by the
presence of these two dead.
Fausto exploded,

"son of bitch are you kidding me? i killed
you!
i had to kill you."

sound cutting in and out like a bad
phone call
"love eternal
like

soul."

his eyes filled and spilled down his face, his
words trapped.

> "can't protect...
> you
> azules
> azules."

They drew into the mirror as Yoli kissed her
clenched fist and released it to him. Only the
quiet remained. They were gone in a blink, with
only an echoing, indecipherable whisper.
Without knocking Annie entered the bathroom,
handed him the phone and left.

"ask no more."

> *...TUS PALABRAS SE VAN AL AIRE Y MIS*
> *LÁGRIMAS AL MAR.*
> *YFP*

CHAPTER 38

Llopis Lantigua was born in Madrid to a British mother and a Borinquen father. She was barely eighteen when her parents forced her to marry the wealthy, aged gentleman who'd whined her and made her laugh. He was not without charm and was different from her boyfriends who liked to cheat on her. It was never her intention to remain with what was little more than sofa sex with a curiosity.

She truly hated their son,

he'd taken everything.

Lantigua's strongest memory of her was at supper. She looked over and blew her child a kiss with her left hand as her other pulled the trigger over her right temple, much of the brain matter landed on Llopis. The head thumped down on her plate, her lips still mouthing,

"i won't love you...

won't love you...

w-won't...

wwoo...wo...."

then nothing.

Her hollow eyes looked upon Llopis, as his peered through her cranium.

Don Lantigua left the country quickly; he made funeral arrangements as the boy sat waiting in a car soon headed for the airport. After landing he was received by a waiting youth and driven to a new island home. Llopis flicked marbles in the yard as his father and the home's patriarch conversed. When he left, he handed the gentleman an envelope of cash. The child was supposed to stay with a family residing on Borinquen. His father promising to come back by the next years' end. They did their part. Sundays he spoke to his dad.

Sundays Don Lantigua spoke to his son. Once a month, the first Monday of the month, barring holidays, he sent the Western Union out.

Then a year and a half later there was no call on Sunday.

Then no money.

A dozen Mondays later, still no money.

The family felt swindled and suddenly the boy became a servant, Llopis was allowed to continue his studies only because he proved an able tutor to the family's youngest child. He was fed last and forbidden to eat if he took too long to cook the meals. If he complained he was beaten. The three sons picked on him unpityingly and the day came when he'd had enough and refused. That night at midnight the parents woke Llopis from his deep slumber. They took him outside and stripped off his clothing and made him stand naked in the dark alone for over an hour, his hands at his side. The father returned with an old rubber hose.

Without warning he sprayed him on the face and body, his thumb and index finger clamped over the end so to increase the pressure of the cold water. When he shut it off, he whipped Llopis with the hose, until the boy, huddled on the ground, could no longer scream out loud. Grabbing him tightly by the elbow he jammed the child into the trunk of the family car and drove. When the car stopped, and the trunk opened, the boy was yanked out and tossed on the road.

in learned spanish,

"ingrato!
on your way back
learn to appreciate
what we do for you."

The father got in the car and drove away. Llopis made his way home before the Sun found him, in time to make breakfast for them.
The abuse grew worse, and he never again objected. That time, and then often, the oldest brother made the boy jerk him off before bed.

It escalated.

Nightly, he raped him in the backyard in the shadows against the mango tree where the family picnicked in the afternoons. That tree had been what inspired the family to learn Spanish and immigrate to Borinquen. He promised to get him thrown out onto the streets if he told anyone.

he did not.

Llopis excelled in school and was eventually saved by a series of forged signatures that allowed him a scholarship, which offered boarding during the year and travel in the summer. That family still resides under that mango tree, they are still listed as missing as are certain neighbors who chose ignore the screams of a child.

Those last years he spent in Lajas, Llopis never saw his father. He went off to Columbia University in New York, where from he later went on to become a Rhodes Scholar. Tipped off by his psychiatrist the Sagrada saw promise in him and recruited Lantigua at the age of twenty-three, there the Nephilim collected him. He was intelligent, ambitious, egotistical, and growing increasingly, but nevertheless superlatively sociopathic.

...UNWANTED

CHAPTER 39

"the blast tore open the truth, bone and
blood everywhere.

     'and then he was fucking dead, he

     died, he's fucking dead.'

it felt thick, like by sudden, wet and
heavy.

couldn't see em, just occasional rustle or
cracked twig. it was usually quiet, quieter
when they were about to do some shit.
but they heard us, fuck man they could
smell the last cigarette you smoked on
your clothes. we could have won that
war, too many rules on us, always so
many damn rules on us, that and assholes
in charge."

             "i heard there were

                so many

             blacks over there that

the dai viets

thought they were being invaded

by africa."

"kid people talk a lot of shit. it's their shit,
i don't know.
yeah there were a lot of blacks and
spanish,
but i knew a ton of country white boys
too.
people bitch when they got nothing going
on.
most don't act.
that's why it coming home was so tough.
people thought it was ok to piss on us. no
respect, job, just something to spit on.
couldn't tell beal, just couldn't.
i mean you're home, finally. and you just
want forget, i mean for a little bit, a little
while at least. not be numb you know, but
maybe normal? i mean i was back like

week... lying my ass off to everybody so
wouldn't know i'd gotten a dishonorable
for falling for a guy.
nobody understands how alone you are
when your world is on fire.
i couldn't sleep in the dark back then
much less at night. rotting parts of your
soul smell worse at night. it was easier for
me pay a guy to use this gritty old gypsy
cab after midnight. it let me hustle while i
tried to get my head straight. but when
your world is off center it takes time to
get it right. this woman gets into my
backseat and tells me she wants to go to
the lower east. that's a big fare and i tell
her that and she's good with it. she's
quiet in the back like the whole ride down.
i'm finally feeling good, a little dignity in
my pocket at days end you know.
we get there and she opens the door and
gets out.

'i ain't paying you jack,'
she says and slams the door and yells as
she walks away,

    'if you got something to say you

    can say it to my peoples.'

with a fucking s. i couldn't even talk i just
watched her walk up to these dudes on
the corner with her arms raised like she'd
won a race while they all hollered shit at
me.

then it got quiet.

i don't really know when it did but it did.

i stopped hearing them and just heard the
crack of bone and windshield. i can
remember stomping the accelerator,
remember this squeaking or like rubbing
coming from under the chassis like when
you run over a basketball. have no idea
how many i hit, but i know it was a couple
of blocks at least before the rubbing
completely stopped. so tired of

everything dumping on me... bronx was always on fire back then. it was easy to get rid of.

showed up at beal's a day later."

...HOME

CHAPTER 40

His head leaning against an elaborate tombstone, Lantigua relieved his bladder on some flowers a family had placed at the grave of a beloved dad who died in the comfort of his family. There were a handful of graves outside the cathedral. He liked to go there and think, about his life, about his father and what would have happened if. Unlike other cities, the NYPD turned a blind eye to this turf war. Unofficially, it supported anything that would stop Lantigua whom they considered responsible for the deaths of three officers. They wanted their revenge too.

He waited quietly, his thoughts circulating. His men hung around nearby uncomfortable with his choice of meditation sites. Killing had been easy but being around they who are dead was frightening, and most of Lantigua's men were merely oversexed boys.

An offensive burning smell permeated, as did
the smoke. The burning of tires became common
ever since the Bodegueros started fighting back.
On the island it is a form of civil disobedience
done mostly when students, workers, and other
citizens were protesting. Llopis smelled it once
before when he put down Aguadulce.

> *revenge is great*
> *if you can pull it off.*

It was humid, the air refused to move, the
clouds above itched to bleed. Midnight came and
the men arrived at the garage across the street.
They were at a bad angle to see her, but the
green angel at the top of the cathedral's steeple
had her back to them.
They'd hit Mickey off with a few bills to get
them keys to the one-tenth street entrance,
Fausto did the same on the one-o-ninth street
side. It was a Tuesday, night, all the cars were in
their respective spots. To look at them, some
worth less than half the value of the hundreds of

dollars in parking fees, you become conscious of exactly how difficult parking is in the city. Lantigua's people took positions behind cars, checking their clips some of them prayed and some wished they called their families, others had no family and believed in nothing. In the end, they waited.

The Bodegueros turned the key. Most would assume that the smart thing to do at that point would be to open fire as soon as they were visible, but that is only wise if one were trying to hold a position or fend off an enemy. A situation like this gets settled decisively...

all out brawl, one winner.

The motor droned as the gate rose exposing the blinding round high beams of an old rust orange Bronco. It rolled forward, gradually, as the men following it dashed in right and left along the entrance sidewalls. They crouched down between cars, careful to place themselves centered to the wheel-well...

as the truck came to a stop and the gate
banged shut against the concrete. The driver's
door opened; he leaped out as somebody fired
the first shots. Many more bullets followed that
punctured the metal, like fingers through dough.

> *shit! i know we tagged him. why didn't
> he go down?*

All went silent for a still second, a slide or two
could be heard...
a cough accompanied by whispers.
Lantigua pressed his face tightly against the
curved angle that hid all but his right eye, hand,
and the barrel between the SUV's rear tire and
muffler.

> *movement.*

Someone was edging closer, Lantigua waited for
the shot, but one of the young cats,

> *one of these fucking kids,*

started emptying a long clip in continuous
oscillating sprays. Lantigua looked back at him
and motioned the others to move forward as the

kid mindlessly provided cover fire. Glass and fiberglass shattered and hit the ground as the kid enacted his gangster movie fantasy. His weapon let off two more rounds even after the Bodeguero's bullet snapped his head back. The single shot sent everyone into a frenzy and spiraling projectiles hurled out of gun barrels. The concrete floors became slippery from the splatter of the wounded.

A unison foot at a time the Bodegueros pushed forward, it was impossible to tell how many were still alive, but their shots hit their targets more often than did those of Lantigua's men. Lantigua's men began to run for the exit, but Fausto's people spit shotgun blasts at anyone who got within three feet of the door and soon nobody was shooting back. Lantigua felt his elbows wetted, he had remained still, absorbing his impending loss. Peeking over he recognized Pincho gasping next to him, the fluids leaving his body fed a growing pool that soaked Lantigua's jeans. Placing his rifle down quickly he dragged the body over himself and played possum, his index finger laid carefully over the trigger. Fausto and the three others checked bodies and shot any survivors.

Sirens began screaming in the distance. It was quicker to pump a few into every body and get out, Lantigua held his breath as he felt the thumping of bullets into the body that blanketed him. For good measure the cars were riddled. He heard the exit-doors open and the men making their way out as they tossed their weapons. Lantigua hurriedly pushed the body off him, getting out was the priority. Carefully he rose to a crouched position and charged to the first beam then the second, two more and he was outside. Cautiously he stretched his neck, his toes on their tips to better enable his sprint. Left foot forward he took off and felt something bite the back of his neck, his body crashed onto the front bumper of a battered hatchback.

Fausto emerged from behind a trunk, discarded his pistol and ran out the door. The Bodegueros scattered,

like roaches,

into the surrounding tenements, across rooftops and alleyways. Police ESU arrived, sirens screaming, to find near two dozen dead and a critically injured suspect later identified as Lantigua, gasping through what was filling his lungs. It is unclear how long it actually took for families to be informed of the deaths; some never were. They lay buried at Potter's Field in numbered plots. Their families never to know that their black sheep were slaughtered. Months passed. Lantigua's stamp,

ghostdancer,

was retired. Hefty fees for making the transition easier, politically, and the Kabuki-Mono was brought into money laundering prospecting for La Bodeguita though Fausto insisted that they adhere strictly to American accounting procedures,

> *japanese could do some creative shit*
> *with the ledgers if you'd let em.*

Those that fought were allowed to profit share,

> *socios.*

Fausto delegated power to these new partners
in the hopes that it would bring greater stability
in the future.

...REVENGE IS GREAT IF

YOU CAN PULL IT OFF

CHAPTER 41

On 96th street looking out over at the Hudson River he heard her voice growl behind him,

"you lied!"

Unable to breathe he turned around to find her cinnamon pools spilling disillusioned tears that tumbled down her face and thundered as they fell. Her skin on her finger's edges could actually be heard rubbing as she signed so much faster than she spoke, in a deep rumble.

"i have your heart and you have mine, yesterday i knew nothing of you, after today nothing exists without you. that is what you said!
hijo de la gran puta!"

hah!

she actually spit on him... pendejo.

As she spoke, she signed ending each phrase
with her index finger and thumb tips touching
as if pricking him with needles.

"like una estupida, maldito coño!

just so i can ugghhh!

como una estupida!

i'm sooo stupid.

you just walked away, like i was
nothing.

you felt it and then stepped on it.

azaroso!

talk, you like talking...

you owe me that! talk pendejo!

say why you couldn't, be a man,

say i didn't matter."

Flustered by her anger she stops signing and
shoves him repeatedly until he falls. Her words,
ever impassioned, vibrated from ever deeper
within her diaphragm she yelled,

until her voice was raspy,

she smacked his forehead with her palm.

"dime coño! dime!"

Fausto looked into her, he stood and reached
for her she shoved him away. He looked left,
then panned right,

the asphalt beneath Angie began to sway. he
fell towards it,

the pendejo forgot to breathe.

He awoke in his bed, exhausted. Annie was
standing beside him sighing in relief. Fausto was
thankful for having her in his life and as he shifted
his head to look at her, he caught focus of the
blue hands.

"how could you be like that!
are you stupid?!"

You could tell how angry Annie was not by her
violence but her speech, it became more
rambled and unpolished.

Digging her nails into his left ear she shoved his
cheek into the pillow.

"what?
are those lil whor-ahs
like that what's her name,
the dirty one
that you like? idiot!"

Infuriated, she stormed off returning instantly
to back-slap him. Accepting, eventually
laughing, he sat up in bed, the stinging finger
marks still imprinted.

his hand over his face

"she wasn't dirty,
her mom made her do...
forget it. annie where is she?

silence.

i know you know."

from somewhere in the house.

"call one of your lil whor-ahs.
you don't want nice.

keep it up

and that lil thing of yours is gonna

shrivel up

and fall off."

> "please stop talking
>
> about my junk.
>
> annie.
>
> i know you know."

stillness.

silence.

> "okay annie i'm
>
> sorry i didn't tell
>
> you!
>
> i'm sorry. fuck man
>
> just tell me."

Thrusting into the room she cracked him across

the mouth. Her finger an inch from his eyes.

"don't yoooou evah curse

at me again you heah me,

you fuckin know bettah.

fucking

know

bettah."

> *exhaling with his hands over his face,*
>> "i didn't curse at you!"

"fausto leonahdo batistah lambargah

I sweah...

I fucking sweah

you better make this right...

boy

you bettah make this right."

Annie drove at speeds that could make anyone
pee their pants. Screeching of the tires
produced a sound and stench that assaulted
the ears and nostrils.

> *slap!*

"yo what the
fuck stop hitting
me!"

The stink perforated as the vehicle screeched
to a stop.

"boy you had bettah get out this car!"

Quickly he forcefully grabbed her face with both
his hands. Almost maniacally he shoved his face
to her cheek pressing his lips.

"i fucking love you
annie.
i don't know where i'd be
without you."

Fausto rushed out of the car and looked up. The
building seemed to extend up forever.

to herself,

"i fucking love you too babyboy,

but please be smarter

than your fathah."

then in an audible tone,

"tell her you're stupid!"

He looked back at Annie.

At the top of lungs he turned and began

screaming.

"angie!!!"

"she's deaf stupid!"

But he continued the long tradition of wooing

common to Latin neighborhoods all over the

world. It went on after Annie called to him.

Without looking he waved her off.

                                        "angie!!!"

His screaming became panicked.

Her hands motioning in elegant flutter,
        "is he actually yelling for me?"
signing as she spoke,

        "yes mi amor,
        that boy
        is downstairs screaming for you."

        "is he dumb mami?"

            sipping a can of soda.
        "all boys are dumb sweetie...

        "ay mami... papi loved him.
        he always said fausto was
        special...
        he really is mami.
        i can't explain it.
        but this?"

yelling continues downstairs.

"mi amor you're barely sixteen. you're
papi, El rest his soul, is gone. i know we
miss him. he was the love of my life. still
is. he was the smartest man i've ever
known, maybe, i don't know maybe the
smartest guy anyone ever met. but that
beautiful boy down there. he...
love makes you feel, not see. this is for
you to decide."

Fausto continued apologizing to the disapproval
of both his vocal chords and the aggravated
audience of windows.

> "he didn't even notice me and my mom
> pass."

"no sweetie. he didn't. i love him.
but he's a boy.
just look at that fool continue making an ass of
himself.

not too many of us will ever be loved like that.
just look at that idiot go."

                                    "angie!"

        "aye angela don't be mean.
        if things have changed for you tell him,
        but i did no raise you to be like that."

"as much as i think he deserves this,
i think your mom is right
it's time to get him.
nati gimme your soda."

            "i'm sorry, i would have brought you
            one, i didn't realize you were thirsty.
            here.
            it still has half."
"perfect."

The chilled carbonation slammed against the
base of his skull.

Exhausted he turned his chin to his chest, his squinting eyes damp and irritated. The cola dripping from his eyebrows onto his eyelashes, he rested his arm on the door an inch from Angie's elbow.

Placing her hand on his head, she rubbed the spot where the can hit.

> "por el amor de Dios
> annie he's already so
> stupid
> and now he's going to get dumber."

Fausto looked up.

"are you done?"

Fixed on her eyes,

> "you wouldn't come."

> "you are handsome my love,
> *sigh*,

but you need to be smarter."

There was some peace as he took her hand.
Gently she pulled her hand from his and after
another pause backslapped him with it.

"hah good for you stupid!"

"can everyone
please stop hitting
me!"

Adjusting his head,

"you must look at me when you speak.
how could you just forget me?"

"too much was
going on. i thought
of you... a lot."

"oh si, que nice,

you thought of me fausto… let me see,

you thought of me soooo much que i

never heard from you. ay si,

yes yes my heart is melting. idiota."

"i was stupid."

"no me digas? so what?"

"can we just get
married?"

Her eyes shot up at him and she partially bit
her lip nervously just as the blue hand of
righteousness again struck down on him.

"you proposed?"

"okay relax… coño!…
uh look angie uhmm.

"i'm not marrying you.

i like you,

very much really,

but we don't know each other yet.

and i'm sixteen."

CHAPTER 42

An afternoon drizzle fell on those who
attended, never really wetting their clothes.
Padre Pirote, the local priest from Ascension
Church where Fausto was baptized that
morning, was to perform the ceremony.
Many years earlier, Yoli tried to get Juni
baptized, as a toddler. When she was told that
she had to take classes to prepare for the
sacrament she told the priest that she did not
need to because they attended mass every
Sunday as a family. He questioned this since he
did not remember seeing them.

> "every sunday, we sit in the back of the
> church father."

Unconvinced but also unwilling to push the
issue he began to speak to her and give the
needed documents when Juni walked in.

"wait for mami in the hall juni."

"oh no please,

let him stay,

after all this is about him."

Juni stood, staring at the priest.

"i can see now that you do

bring him to church a lot.

i am sorry i doubted you,

look at how focused on me he is.

you are teaching him well mrs. batista."

Juni tugged at his shirt.

"leave the curita alone juni,

yoli said between her teeth.

"it's fine really,

tell me juni is it?

what would you like to ask me?"

"are you a doctor?"

262

"doctor?

ohhhh doctor.

no juni i am not a doctor.

i am a priest, a cura.

do you know what a priest

or a cura is?"

Juni shook his head no.

Yoli, embarrassed, her hand over her face stood

up picked up her son and left.

...DEVOUT

CHAPTER 43

twenty-nine months
and a warm day later.

The nuptials were held under the midday Sun's in Central Park in a lagoon of flora. The location was off of the Museum Mile and could be seen from the windows of Mount Sinai Hospital. A woman afflicted with Pica somehow managed to retch hunks of soap through a slanted window and down a half-dozen floors, all of which fell into the spray fountain centered in the driveway. Countless bubbles formed then hovered over the wedding party, each one inimitably refracting light.

Annie suggested that they recite their own vows, but they declined and instead agreed on traditional vows. As they knelt before the altar Angie and Fausto began simultaneously signing to one another. It seemed as though everyone understood what was meant, despite Fausto's mumblings. They become lost in feeling as the ground respired underneath them. Their first wed-locked kiss as husband and wife resonated sempiternally. When the kiss ended, the music and celebration began. Angie wandered about, smiling politely as the guests congratulated her. Bobby, Fausto's best man, leapt around excitedly until he bumped into a speaker knocking it on its' face. The vibrations pumped into the ground. Angie's smile grew more organic, and she began to subtlety move. Fausto noticed and quickly ran around from speaker to speaker pushing each one down. Angie began to dance, her eyes locking onto her husband until he joined her. They continued into the night. Annie's eyes watered, as the young couple drove off after the reception. Alone and pensive, she wandered into the bridal tent. Most brides would have taken hours to get ready, but it took Angie only effortless minutes. Refusing to wear shoes, or any footwear for that matter, she tossed on the elegant long white dress and some lipstick. Annie stood silently, looking around, wondering what she would do now that her Faufi was a man with a wife.

an unfamiliar voice,

"thank you
for all that you have done for him."

she turned,

Annie recognized her from pictures she'd seen over the years. Even in death she was beautiful.

"come, sit."

She radiated as Annie stared as she sat next to her amazed at how there she seemed to be.

"he could have never held on to his heart
without you."

"why are you here?"

"i have always been here,
today you noticed."
and she was gone.

Annie sat, overcome with a buzz of tranquility
that had always escaped her.

...SEMPITERNAL

CHAPTER 44

"Time present and time past
Are both perhaps present in time future,
And time future contained in time past.
If all time is eternally present
All time is unredeemable."

> *Burnt Norton, Four*
> *Quartets*
> *T.S. Eliot*

Existence can be broken down into realities, transpositioning ones, all of which wield heavy influences over the two cross-worlds known to us as earth,

one evolving and one devolving.
The supernal higher worlds which are made up of seven superfluous Dwellings, the mid-worlds which are made of nine Dwellings where one must accrue understanding and the lesser worlds which are made up of seven Dwellings

where cold, despair and torment reign,

chaos unceasingly imploding.

Entities can transcend, but it occurs rarely
since memories and beliefs impair elevation.
When El conceived this universe, he knew from
studying his creation that purity will nearly
always become tainted, and truth will always be
distorted. There are twenty-three descending
units all angled perfectly to meet like a sliced
flan and intersect through our physical world,
which is one of two,

the other is asymmetrical.

He structured the unearthly to deal with the
many different degrees or absences of justice
that compose the behavior of both humanity
and its' metaphysical brethren.

Yoli drifted, patiently learning to navigate, more
so opportunistically managing to watch over
her child. The moments that passed existed in a
state of silent loneliness, focused only on her
son. It was only after so much mortal time that

she saw the fall of her murderer. All dead knew of his landing because a dramatic vibration shook the worlds, and the rivers overflowed. In the Middle Dwellings they who are dead exist in a state of nothingness, a quest to formulate questions in a place of infinite answers. They float, endlessly, over unsettled bodies of water and lands they could never set foot upon. He was the first to actually touch the surface, the event sent a ripple through existence. Countless souls began to feel a tremendous force push them to the red-clay-crust and they began walking, often through each other, disoriented from the change. The rivers of souls grew dense as it became damned with confusion.

Leo lay on the crust, watching as all walked into and out of him, he was there for a mortal year before he realized he was dead. Overtime the remorse that he bared throughout the worlds only intensified and souls were forced to crawl

and sometimes slither from the weight. Yoli
observed him,

> *from afar,*

she knew he would discover her inevitably, and
wondered often what would come of it. She
did not fear him, even after. There were still
numerous souls who could float and Yoli was
one of them. She took to hovering just over
and behind Leo, in trepidation of a possible
encounter.

> *then,*

on a moment on a day when Yoli lingered in
memories, she felt a grabbing at her legs. The
moment she touched land the grounded souls
were flung passed the clouds leaving only Leo
and her as the crust's inhabitants. Leo was on
his belly holding her feet to the ground.

"death parted us, let go."

> "please

stop hating me."

She stopped struggling and in one motion broke free from his hold, here she was as strong as he was.

> angrily she put her hand around his
> throat, her thumbnail to the center.

"you stole my life!
you took my life with my son.
i hate you
you infected our son."

> he was unable to look at her,
>
> she felt for him.
>
> santa marta's disappointment
> only festered further.
>
> but love is warm,
> even bad love.

She pushed him away.

"i am not for you.

i cannot grant you peace."

"if there is a chance..."

He then looked to the worlds above and for judgement. Leo begged for El to sentence him immediately, and mercilessly. Offended, he was furiously looked upon. Leo was to spend twelve times one thousand moments in the darkest of the shadows without the release of a scream. If he dared scream, it would begin again.

it would begin, many times.

Upon completion of the sentence, he would be forgiven in the eyes of El and the Elders. Yoli was thrusted away from him, a tremendous shadow overcame him, she watched as the manifested multitude of gold, green, and red scaled demons bit and dug talons into him, lifting him then driving him into the crust,

through the remaining mid-worlds to the
entrance of the damned and finally to its'
lowest chamber,

    xibalba.

...GRAVITY

CHAPTER 45

There are many childlike creatures in hell,

whether they are or not is

unbeknownst to us.

Leo looked into the pools as the souls that

danced, unwillingly,

to the high-pitched piercing gases made moan,

escaping the walls. Thunderous globs of the

molten glass slammed down and sprayed

countless burning shards that pierced their

remembered flesh and then rattled uniformly

around them. Screams were deafening and the

blistering cold was more mean than bitter, it

smelled of nothing and embers that issued no

warmth seared across the sky. Living tornados,

threading ropes of fire, gobbled up stones, and

defeated souls, flinging them onto the altars of

the tormentors.

As he turned, he saw the shadow of his own

inflictor rolling over him holding in one hand the

clamps that would keep him and in the other the dulled tools that would torture him.

El looked at Yoli and the pain that enveloped her.

She would not question.

...BURN

CHAPTER 46

The couple arrived at the hotel room; Angie
held Fausto's hand tightly. She was anxious
about what was to happen, she'd made him
wait. She'd wanted to, but she chose to make
him wait and not for moral, religious, or
traditional reasoning. Becoming deaf at a young
age, Angie had been underestimated and
undervalued by most. There was time for sex,
and she would decide when.

She looked at him, wondering how many women
there'd been. Would the whole experience be
awkward?

A night before and much to Chito's disgust, her
mother had taken the time to tell her the
details of her wedding day. Beal had been
courting Natividad Mirabal for two years before
she finally paid any attention to him. They
dated secretly for a year before he went to her
father and presented himself as the man who

wished to marry Nati. He told him that they were in love and that they wanted to spend the rest of their lives together. The father became furious stating that his daughter was worthy of more.

Santa Marta,

la dominadora,

took a liking to her despite the distaste she held for the girl's father. Discovering her too late to have exerted the type of influence she would have liked; she guided the environment to favor her. Her love was strong, and she promised Nati in a dream that occurred when she was less than asleep that her first child if born a girl would be to her like a daughter and that she would teach her in the ways forgotten. Beal was a well-spoken seventeen-year-old, he pleaded to continue seeing Nati swearing that he would continue improving himself until he was worthy of her. The father conceded on the condition that he would always respect her virtue. Months passed and Beal became more acceptable in the eyes of Don Mirabal, so much so that he allowed Beal to be her escort at her quinceañera. The celebration was grand considering how humble they were. Countless photographs were taken and Nati looked beautiful in her dress,

that dress.

As the festivities began to wind down, the guests began wondering where the young couple was. No one had seen them in some time and her father and his brothers prepared to go out,

machetes behind the door,

and find them. Then they walked in, her hair undisturbed, and her dress unwrinkled. Doña Mirabal whispered to her husband that they had probably gone outside to steal some kisses,

harmless.

The father walked over to his daughter and reluctantly coughed up a smile, he then walked over to Beal and shook his hand for the first time. Beal became overcome with joy; he smiled as he shook the hand. When he did the entire room somehow focused on him, more specifically his smile.

Caught in between his two front teeth was a short brown pubic hair.

Everyone saw it and Don Mirabal angrily walked away as the crowd became hushed with shock followed by uproarious laughter. Nati looked at her lover and then whispered in his ear informing him. His smile slid away, the couple now aware of their slip, stood there hand in hand,

frozen.

The father returned with a revolver, placed it snugly against Beal's tear duct and gave his permission to marry his daughter. Doña Mirabal led the local priest out to the center of the room and the ceremony was performed.

Angie chuckled to herself as she remembered.

They arrived at the door, and she held her breath as she was carried over the threshold. She kissed her husband and then went into the bathroom.

The new bride ran a hot bath, and the room quickly became clouded. Her stomach knotted; Angie sat at the tub's edge. She removed a small stuffed pouch from her bag and opened it, from it she pulled many colorful flower petals that she patiently crushed and submerged into the water. While she did it, she prayed for happiness and nothing more. Then she took out a tiny jar of honey and cupped out some of it. The young Mrs. Batista slowly massaged it between her fingers as she allowed the faucet's warm water to run over her hand.

She entered into the bath and laid back peacefully as the multitudes of petals danced over and around her body drunk on the sweet water they were drowning in. A spoonful of time later she rose and prepared to know her husband.

Fausto undressed immediately,

you'd think he'd wash up.

He had bedded women over the years, but
none but one other had he known admitted
affection for, let alone love. The selfish sex he'd
known was never more than eye gesture or
quick conversation away. They were women
who wanted him because of the money, the
daughters of a few mothers who prodded their
beautiful girls to get something they wanted,
the older women who just wanted him,

and serena.

Most were compensated in one way or another.
None ever meant much to him having learned of
the physical act at a young age. Fausto was
about to commit an act of vulnerability.

He could hear her fussing about in the
bathroom and he imagined how scared she had
to be. The bathroom door opened, and she
rushed towards the bed's end,

282

not towards him.

Her nightgown was simple and flowed rhythmically down her skin from her shoulders to her thighs. She did not face him,

her husband... husband!

In something reminiscent of a lotus position Angie sat there frozen, forcing her breathing. Fausto watched her carefully almost cautiously; he touched her arms sliding only the ends of his fingers down to her forearms and back. He smelled her curled hair and the neck that it rested on awakening her skin with his lips tasting its' sweetness with the edge of his tongue. Cradling her chin as if fragile, he brought her to his eyes. Fausto looked into her, her expression, and smiled as he held her. Excitement and fear caused her to perspire, the short cotton gown clung to her moistened skin as he moved her dark curled hair, undid the bows on the straps and tasted her smooth tense brown shoulders with each kiss finally coaxing her out of hesitation as her palms found comfort on the top of his head. Her lips pouted and trembling, eventually a near primal howl escaped from deep within her diaphragm. Pleasure overran flesh until the night stalked the daylight.

...SWEET FIFTEEN

CHAPTER 47

Yoli alone walked the crust. She was held down
by the weight on her heart, any soul could
share the skies with her only Leo could walk the
crust with her. Her prayers were constant and
not unheard.
The moments motioned clumsily,
one then another.
From under a passing silhouette,

the moon? maybe,

she'll never tell,

hunched over wet and trembling, he returned.
Yoli found him and wanted to hold him but did
not. She tried to calm him, but the madness
still slid over his form.

then silence. silence. silence.

Until he was then still,
finally, realized his surroundings, he looked at
her.

A loud cry streaked,
the one he held for so long and through so
much.
It killed birds in their nests.

                              "if i have to return
                         to that place a thousand
                             times... i will... i will."

Memories flaked from her temples until they
were raw and more easily overtaken by feeling.
They stood on the fabric of the universe before
an audience of souls.
Their hands clasped together.

                                        ...NOW TAKE

CHAPTER 48

"If I sinned I sinned only against myself
but you,
immortal one,
sin against all that was is and shall be."

Alberich, Das Rheingold

Richard Wagner

The one in the 401 Powers of the Right, and the one in 201 Powers of the Left, Satanas, the Great Satanas, The Weaver of Sin, Great Deceiver.

blah blah blah,

is an egotistical and unyielding asshole with tasty supernatural icing.

He is brilliant and alluring, inebriatingly appealing to both woman and man alike. A beautiful entity.

prettiest motherfucker

you ever did see

charming to the push of seduction, he loves
nothing, but desires everything.

Still, Satanas is not the lone leader of the
Misifoos. Azules remains the only of the fallen
angels ever to challenge Satanas and his
Misifoos. She was the first angel that Satanas
conned into turning against El and she blamed
him squarely for her tumble. The ambitious
seraph was obsessed with leaving the great
opposer powerless and exposed. Profoundly, she
believed that by extinguishing Satanas, she
would be catapulted back home.

> *home.*
> *home is a cave.*
> *a massive cave with slumber*
> *spaces carved into in gleaming*
> *polished walls. it features*
> *an opening at the right rear of its'*
> *concave ceiling large enough for*
> *the moon to enter when it is*

weary and needs to become anew.

lavender grows horizontally on

all the stays under foot. it is

where the most young go to wait

and play before they return to

life.

their scars and burns still

visible.

she missed it.

them.

every infectious laughing,

every tiny grip around her

fingers.

With countless bitter angels at the ready, Azules effectively split the lesser realms into two, controlling three of the seven worlds and fighting to bring forth the end of days believing that by crushing Satanas before the intended time she would be reinstated and brought back into El's embrace. Azules failed to realize that time frames exist for His reasoning and that by challenging it she was in effect challenging El. Her Misifoos warred with Satanas' demons constantly weakening the devil's control over the earth and strengthening her own. The goal was to rob him of the Apocalypse, to strip the earth and all the realms of his existence. The uprising was ripping through the lesser worlds and now Azules was laying the groundwork on the cross world. She would not await the fulfillment of prophecy or parable. She began constructing a web of servants. The conspiracy was to bring forth the end of days without Satanas's involvement. The great deceiver was to be cheated of his infamous destiny. When the Nephilim became aware of the conspiracy, they worked to restore order. Unfortunately, their methods were too iniquitous. They also hadn't realized or considered that El had plans for Azules, plans that even though he was not aware of it were centered on Fausto.

...PRETTIEST MOTHERFUCKER YOU EVER DID SEE

CHAPTER 49

*"I tell you one must have chaos in one to give
birth to a dancing star."*

Friedrich Nietzsche

Her pregnancy was exhausting. Angie was tiny
framed, and the extra weight and strain wore
her to the point where she only seemed to be
functional for fifteen minutes at a time and that
was seemingly reserved for eating. Fausto
often teased her by saying she would probably
sleep through childbirth unless it happened to
coincide with a craving. Her belly was huge by
the fifth month,

always tired.

She was easily agitated, and just hungry. Her
belly grew so that Fausto was forced to reposition the bed so he could watch television in
bed without straining to see over her belly.
This ended when she went into labor in her

seventh month.

Angie was prepped for the epidural before deciding to refuse the pain medication. It was the thirty-third hour of labor when she finally was ready to push. Angie squeezed Fausto's hand with crushing force as she pushed out the life that had resided in her. The grip did not allow him to reach the video camera that she had made him bring to record the event. She pushed and Jaiden Soledad Batista was finally introduced headfirst into the world at 7 pounds 13 ounces complete with a head full of hair accentuated by a white streak. They named her as she made her way out from the womb,

when she was crowning to be exact.
The child screamed out in a healthy cry and then vacated.

Emptied, the infants' skin cooled, quickly as the doctor and nurses encircled, trying desperately to tempt life back into the tiny corpse. Fausto crumpled,

> *dizzied,*
>
> *his groin pushing towards his*
>
> *lungs,*

he remained folded.

The air,

paused,

paused.

> *choking,*
>
> *throat,*
>
> *where's angie.*

Clenching her hand he held it to his face, the tips of her fingers wetting. Angie squinted in anguish as Jaiden Soledad Batista was pronounced at 1:11am. A nurse sponged off the body, wrapped it in a soft cotton blanket and gave it to them.

Machines off, the room remained soundless, the staff believing it better to leave the young couple to mourn.

Angie vanished. Flesh slid from bone. Her souls caged in the skeletal remnants.

Fausto inserted his arm under the swaddled
bundle.
He did it without thinking.
He couldn't think over the screaming flinging
from his chords.
He didn't want to drop her, but he couldn't hold
on to her.
A nurse took the infant corpse from his arms,
it didn't stop Fausto from screaming. Outside,
the doctor informed Annie of the happening,
she sat shaking in disbelief.

"som... something is happening!"

The staff rushed in. Her exhaling outpaced her
inhaling.

"mrs. batista,
it's afterbirth,
the placenta,
i'm sorry.
i am deeply sorry."

The doctor worked to spare Angie the pain and trauma of further disappointment when a nurse yelled,

"doctor! i see feet!"

She was delivered feet first seven pounds thirteen ounces with a full head of hair and a white streak. The newborn began to cry intensely long and hard then paused only to breathe in new air and release it in a deafening wail. The child was placed in Angie's arms.

she blurted out jaiden soledad.

Fausto was too overwhelmed to protest. He was jubilant and woeful, hugging his wife as she held their newborn. El watched from the door and left drawing no attention.

Annie entered the room followed by Margaro Osmin.

Fausto slipped over to his firstborn.

color and warmth fading.

Unable to lift he caressed her, kissing the top of

her head, the swaddled corpse feeling all at once vacuous and disconnected from the world empty leaving the air thinning.

"i can feel how gone she is."

He then walked back towards Angie and the baby followed by Fausto. He revised baby Jaiden carefully; he told them that she would be strong in mind and action.
The newborn Jaiden arrived at her new home two days later one day after the first-born Jaiden was buried in a grave next to a cherry plum tree on the property. The house smelled sweet and light, Annie had been cleaning with white ammonia and Mistolin all day,
unsafe mix but she loves that shit.
She was excited about becoming a godmother and did everything she could think of to make the baby's homecoming pleasant. Jaiden slept as soon as she was placed in her crib. Fausto and Angie fell soon after.

Late that night, Fausto was awoken by whispers, when he looked to the crib there was a silhouette playing with the baby. He did not interrupt them though he deeply wanted to be involved in the playtime.

Watching from the edge of his bed, he listened to how Jaiden responded. Angie was startled awake by the happiness and shushed by Fausto's finger over her lips.

"that's my mother."

"i know her...
i mean... before,
she came to me when papi died."

Jaiden fell asleep and Yoli faded.

...JAIDEN SOLEDAD

CHAPTER 50

He is darkness shined upon, a Morning Star, and she is not written.

...SHE IS NOT WRITTEN

CHAPTER 51

"up on the temple,

hurry up so we can clean up and go."

       "nah wait

       i thought you was gonna do it."

"memo what the fucks the difference?

anyway

you the one who told me henli was talking."

       "he was,

       it was him."

"then shut the fuck up and shoot…

ahhh fuck it! gimme."

Memo exhaled in relief and closed his eyes as
Fausto snatched the pistol away.

"you're a shit memo."

        "what?"

"i said you're a shit.
i know all about you
and your little brother.
fuck man
you've been with me for years."

                "you got it wrong,
                        it's henli.
                i saw him talking to the
              jailermen in a room at the
            station. i heard him telling
        them about the shit in the back
              of the pet shop."

"really? wait shit that's right they knew exactly
where to look and henli missed that pick up. he
never showed. did you henli? even the shop
owner didn't know.

300

memo nodding nervously in

agreement.

take that shit out of his mouth.

henli gasped at the air as the sock

was removed.

henli do you wanna explain yourself,

tell me

why didn't you

pick up the package that day?"

"what fucking package!?

what the fuck is going on!?"

"oh yeah that's right.

i forgot to get word to henli about the

pick up.

only you knew

well you and the law.

cut him loose,

sorry henli

i needed him to admit it."

The blood spurted as memo collapsed and

sobbed,

his brother Luis' left boot tumbling after the

slanted thrust of the machete.

The foot still inside the sock that remained

snuggly inside the shoe.

Papito further raised the volume on the TV as

Memo bawled. Fausto sliced through the nylon

string holding Henli's hand down and then

dropped the wet cleaver on his lap.

"you were gonna let me kill him.

what i kill him

you snitch and boom

you gonna run shit?

rats hide,

steal,

make us sick.

they don't run shit."

Fausto grabbed the boot and hit Memo across

the bridge of his nose as Luis went into shock

while still holding the pressure on his tourniquet.

"is that it you little fuck?"

In a rage,

   primal,

he beat him with it until the gurgling stopped and Memo's face no longer resembled a man.
   ring.

"keep him quiet i gotta answer this. yeah...
give me a few to tie up
some loose ends and i'll bounce over."

The muffled shot was louder than it should have been, but not loud enough to disturb. His head leaning to the left, his mouth open as blood spilled onto the tarp. Luis was still alive, but Henli began hacking him up anyway.

"clean up.

wrap them up and get rid of them."

    "yo faust,

    you think maybe papito can do it.

    i mean i'll help him load it in the

    car, but this my weekend with my kid

    yo.

    you know how his moms be."

        "aguanta, hold on,

        aguantatemardito gordo…

        faust,

        as it is i gotta

        handle that shit over in

        corona. i got like thirty

        forty minutes or else we

        lose that. i mean it's a

        couple of bricks,

        we can't flake.

and this guy always got an excuse,

with his fucking jetset kid or some

other bullshit."

"nah it's not like that."

"ya'll shitting me?

there's a crew of what a couple dozen

and you couldn't put one of them to handle

two bricks?

and you what the fuck!

your kid?

that girl's been playing you forever.

fucking accept it.

seven month old preemies

are not nine pounds

you dumb fuck.

look load all this shit in my car

i'll take care of it.

do it

then get away from my fucking sight!

and henli enough!

they need to go in a bag not a fucking
jar."

        jetset babies are eggs fertilized,
        often anonymously,
        in nightclub bathroom stalls. paternity
        often proved… complicated.

        …I'M SURE SHE WAS ON THE PILL

CHAPTER 52

Fausto walked to his car.

they fucking left lights on,

deep down he prayed that it started. When it
did, he exhaled the dozen or so curses he'd
been grinding in his teeth.

The car pulled up to Nati's building, Fausto got
out and placed the baby in her protective seat.
Focused on her actions rather than Fausto's
lips, she banged on the trunk

"abre!,

i'm going to toss the baby bag in,",

Scrambling out of the car and over to her.

"no no the trunk
is full of junk.
just put it in the
backseat."

They got in and pulled away. Muttering under
his breath,

> "i keep telling
> you to get your
> damn license.
> i can't always
> stop what i'm
> doing to come
> get you."

Angie breathed.

more like a sigh.

"i never thought
it was such a sacrifice.
please
forgive me for wanting a moment."

> "you sure your
> deaf?

你know i have
to work."

"veng aqua!
we never finished our
discussion about your retirement.
and don't think you are not gonna pay for that."

"not the time angie."

"que?, move your head to me."

"can I drive? please!"

"fausto look.
the baby is about to be baptized,
i think that is the time for you to quit.
there is more than enough money
and it's
only a matter of time
before you get caught.
your daughter deserves

to have a father that is

not some common criminal."

> "i'm really not
>
> common."

"oh well excuse

the fuck out of me mister capone!

look,

as your wife

i have a right to my husband here and

alive!"

> "ang, you know cursing
>
> doesn't work for you,
>
> so don't do it anymore.
>
> quitting takes time."

surprised,

"do you really want to quit?"

310

"what i want means

nothing,

just drop it...

please..."

Then there was silence.

Only the sounds of a slumbering infant.

The road.

Passing car.

Sign.

Light.

Car.

Car.

Car.

"how was your mom?"

Adjusting his head forward in order to be
noticed.

"how's your mom?"

"fine and she sends her love as always.

i'm starting to think she prefers you to me…

fausto smirks,

wait. hold on. did you just smile?

oh my gosh.

you totally have a crush on my mom!"

"whoa!!!

i do not

have a crush on

your mom"

"so my mother is not pretty?"

"what? no no

your mom is hot.

like crazy

sin in a can hot.

any guy hell anybody would…

at that moment fausto

peripherally noticed the intense focus

of his wife, on his lips,

his face.

i mean…

                                        like for an
                              outsider you know
                                          uhmm."

She stared without words.
Then
she burst out laughing her forehead to her
shoulder.

"it's ok mi amor
my mama is hot.
everybody sees it.
i'm hot even i know that.
and you see her
in the rearview mirror sleeping like an
angel. baby
she's gonna be hot too
and every boy
i'm sorry,
everybody is going to notice."

                              "how is that funny?

why would...

why would you put that in my head?"

pulling into the driveway. angie
getting out and grabbing the baby.

"mi amor. come on.

every woman was somebody's little girl at some
point in time.

or did you think all those cueritos

you've been with over the years just magically

appeared?

...aren't you coming?"

"give me a few
i have to finish up it'll be quick."

"ta bien, but hurry."

She kissed him and Fausto turned the wheel. He
watched her go inside, their baby in arms.
The truth was that he liked looking at her. When
he arrived at the garage on one-o-eighth street

off Amsterdam Ave. several workers ran to the
car as he got out. While he talked to a recently
promoted manager named Leni, the other
workers quickly removed the well-wrapped
sacks from his trunk and hurriedly began
washing and detailing the car,

> *steam the fabric.*

> "leni i need to meet
> this week, spread the
> word."

He got back into the car,

> *still a little damp,*

and drove home. Upon arrival he parked the car,
but left the engine running with the heat full
blast,

> *it'll probably be out of gas by*
> *morning. used to be able to just*
> *dump the car,*
> *but angie would notice.*

As he entered the house, he walked slowly as

to not be too noisy. He looked down with every step careful not to step on any statues that should scamper by,

strangely none did.

Fausto went upstairs and towards his bedroom. He could hear his beloved snoring heavily and laughed to himself wondering how such a little woman could make such an offensive noise. Still very careful of the night floor's inhabitants he heard a scratching noise in the nearby darkness. Quickly, he turned on the hallway light, one of them a small chubby lion statue was desperately clawing at Jaiden's door, as he stepped towards it the figurine turned to him and Fausto could actually see its' panic. He opened the door to find the moonlight illuminating a pockmarked faced girl holding his sleeping daughter, her lips colorless like her skin, suckled from the infant's belly. Confused, he flicked on the light switch. Lifting her head slowly, her mouth dripping the pilfered

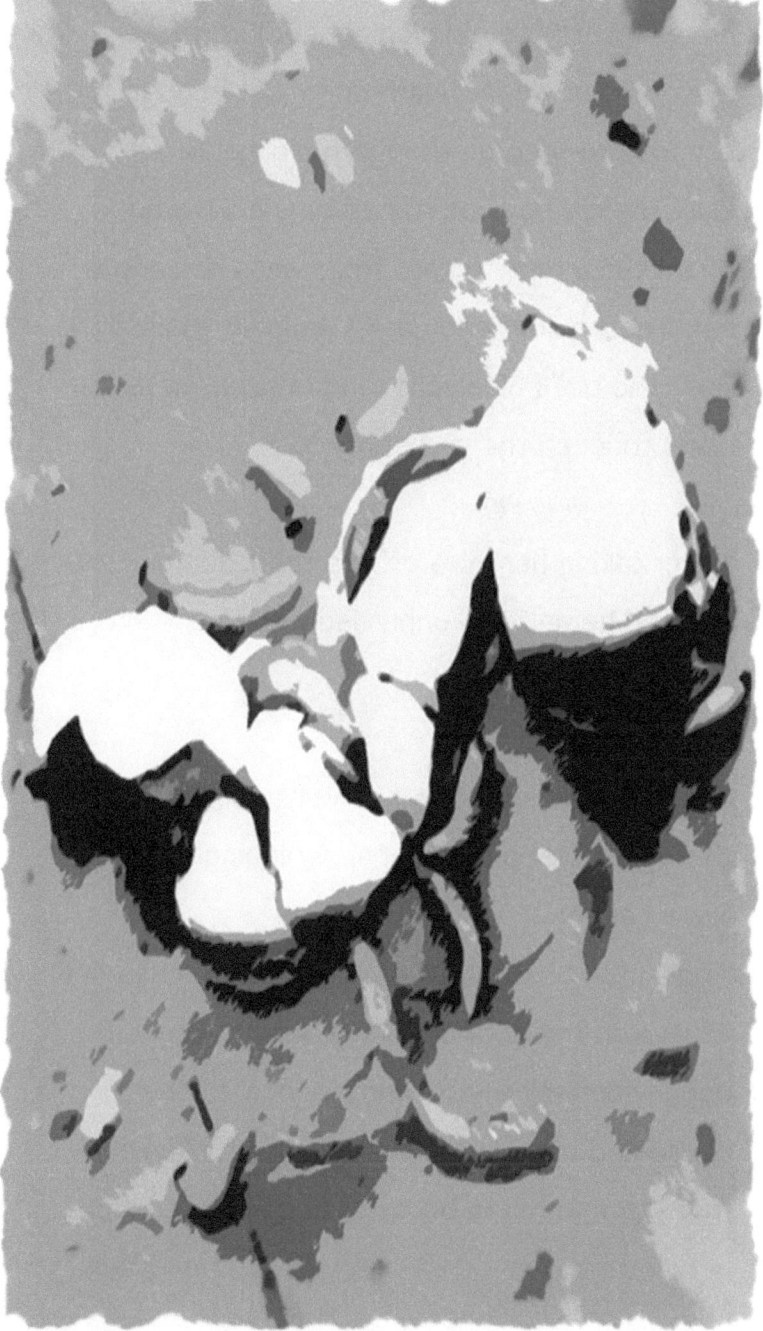

nourishment; the girl giggled, her berry blue eyes void of white. She floated just enough for her toes to drag on the floor, alongside her hair. The chubby lion roared at the girl who threw the infant, Fausto froze once he caught her. His shoulder and neck slamming against the wall. The girl's blue split tongue exposed as her heels touched the carpeting.

giggling.

Never taking her eyes off the child, she partially lowered herself and unhurriedly walked backwards,

like a crab,

until she reached the windowsill and leapt through it, her platinum hair wrapping around like a cocoon.

Angie stumbled out of her bed and room to find Fausto on the floor clutching Jaiden. Annie began screaming from another part of the house and baby in arms, he bolted to Annie's room to find her in bed. Her body twisted and covered with scratches and bite marks, on her back the name Azules was written in dried blood. The floor was riddled with crushed animal statues and the house suddenly smelled like burning feces. Angela ran to the phone and called Osmin who instructed her not to disturb anything. He arrived some twenty minutes later to find Fausto still and Annie unconscious. In her father's arms Jaiden was peacefully asleep, fluid dripping her from her stomach. Angela swept up the valiant figurines as Osmin examined Annie, the bites looked small. He mouthed to Angela to bring him some cigarettes and beer. Immediately, he aggressively smoked and drank, all the while flicking florida water on the corners of the room, until Anaisa arrived and assumed his body.

i don't get it either.

Upon her arrival the stereo turned on and began blasting percussion rhythms, she,

she,

danced then placed her hands on Annie's' entire wrenched body and slid them up and down while it crackled and straightened. About one hour later the motion was over her spine, erasing the words. Anaisa held an egg and passed it over the body stopping only to pull out long metallic blue needles from Annie's joints and temples.

"she sleep, i will now help him,

por favor otro huevo."

She went over to him with the egg in hand and drove it into his forehead. Fausto dropped to his knees as Anaisa took the baby and handed her to Angie. He heaved over and over again until he began to choke finally coughing up a snake with clear scales. It was long and it raised its' head to hiss at them. Anaisa crushed it under her left heel, and it collapsed into a mound of dead maggots over a cracked egg containing the skeleton of a smaller serpent.

"she has come for you.